PLAINS PARAMOUR

Jack Hastings panted as he made the noose. He stared down at the groaning man. Doubt clouded his brain but he quieted it. This wasn't killing. It's never killing during a war. It's doing a job that has to be done, and this was a war.

"You killed them," Hastings said as he knelt and slipped the noose around Fields's neck. "You killed my parents! You raped my mother! You didn't think anybody was left but I saw it. I saw it all!"

He pulled the rope tight. Fields coughed and opened his eyes. "What—what—"

Hastings smiled. "You're getting what you deserve, Yankee!"

Lester Fields's voice was scratchy. "You're the one! You've been killing my friends!"

He laughed. "Yeah. And you're gonna join 'em—in hell!"

SPUR #29

PLAINS PARAMOUR

DIRK FLETCHER

LEISURE BOOKS NEW YORK CITY

*Thanks to Scott Cunningham
for his contribution to this book.*

A LEISURE BOOK®

October 2005

Published by

Dorchester Publishing Co., Inc.
200 Madison Avenue
New York, NY 10016

ISBN 0-8439-2763-1

Printed in the United States of America.

Visit us on the web at www.dorchesterpub.com.

CHAPTER ONE

I'm gonna kill him.

The thought pounded in his brain, blasted through every nerve in his body. He deserves to die. He *has* to die for what he did. It's justice. It's everything that's right.

He followed the man through the darkened streets of Quintoch, Kansas. The saloons were quiet and all decent citizens had long ago gone to bed. But not that one. He'd been out drinking, carousing, going over old times with his murdering friends.

It'd be the last time he did that!

Mark Inglewood couldn't quite keep his eyes open. He stumbled down the rutted, dusty street, knees bending, muscles sluggish. Okay, so maybe he shouldn't have had that last drink. But hell! He'd be home soon enough, safe in bed next to his woman who'd be snoring away.

He'd grab her, wake her up, want her. She'd turn over and refuse to touch him when she smelled the

5

liquor on his breath. Inglewood sighed. Some
things never changed.

But he couldn't help the drinking, he thought,
staring at the shimmering crossroads ahead. He
had to pack down all that whiskey. Things were so
boring since the great war ended. There was
nothing to do. No battles to be won. No goddamn
fun!

Inglewood's stomach rebelled at the bitter liquid
he'd poured into it. He felt it heaving, threatening
to come up. He stooped over a hitching post, stared
at the inky water of the trough and waited.
Nothing. Feeling better, the tall, muscled man
groaned and lurched toward Settler's Avenue. It
wasn't far now.

Reeling forward, his feet refusing to work
properly, Mark Inglewood heard something
behind him. Normally he'd turn to see what it was
but he just didn't feel like it. Besides, the town was
safe. Never any problems here. No robberies, no
killings, no shootouts—no fun!

He made it to Settler's Avenue. The cool night air
had finally cleared his head. Mark straightened his
back and moved toward his house. Just half a block
down. Just half a block to his wife and the kid and
sleep.

Half a block.

The dark figure twisted the rope. He worked
quickly as he followed the drunken man, forming
the knot as best he knew how. Hurry, he told
himself. His shaking hands fumbled. He silently
cursed himself and his pain-racked brain, pulled
the rope apart and started over.

He'd practiced so long that night, waiting for that damn man to leave the saloon. It just figured he'd be the last one out.

Mark Inglewood had stopped moving.

That gave him just enough time to complete the long, wrapped knot with the loop at the end. He ran his fingers over the rough hemp, checking it. It should work.

The sleeping town was lit with thin moonlight, but the silver glow turned to red in his mind. He shook his head, trying to quench the internal fire that boiled within his skull. It didn't work. Whenever he thought about it, about what had happened, it seemed his head was about to explode. He couldn't stop the pain.

Don't worry about that now. Just do it!

His prey had turned off the main street. He was nearly home. Time to act.

The knotted rope slapped softly against his thigh as he hurried toward him. Fifty feet. Thirty. Twenty. He pulled the heavy iron hammer from the back pocket of his overalls.

Mark Inglewood stopped and turned to face him. "Hey, boy! What're you doin' up so late?" he asked, his words alcohol-slurred.

"Just this!"

The hammer went up and pounded down. Inglewood groaned and dropped to the street. His assailant returned the hammer to his pocket, threw the rope over his shoulder and lifted the unconscious man by his armpits. He dragged him to the tree behind the small house, working slowly, making no noise, ignoring the agony that surged through his head.

He knew the branch was high enough, he'd checked that while waiting. The man lugged Mark Inglewood to the base of the neatly-stacked firewood. He took a deep breath and surged into action.

Lengthen the loop. Push it around the head. Pull it tight until it cuts into the neck.

He threw the other end of the rope over the highest clear branch and hauled Mark Inglewood to the top of the five-foot high woodpile. It moved under his boots so he paused until he regained his footing. He quickly checked the length of the rope and the height. It should work.

He jumped down and secured the loose end of the rope around a thick, dead branch. It was taut.

The ache in his head lessened. His heart banged. Sweat squeezed from every pore in his body. He lifted the man to his feet and slapped his face.

Mark grunted and opened his eyes. "What's—what's going on here?"

"Goodbye!"

He pushed. The drowsy man swung out on the rope, legs kicking, arms flailing as the tension settled around his neck. Strangled cries blasted out from his throat. Inglewood swung back and forth in a slow arc, his boots a foot from the ground, gasping as he slowly died.

Watching from on top of the woodpile, the other man sighed. The headache was gone. He looked into the branches of the tree, smiled and slowly walked away. He turned back just once to see Mark grabbing the noose, frantically trying to dislodge it from his neck.

With any luck, Mark Inglewood would be dead in a half-hour.

Spur McCoy opened the telegram again as he sat in the barber's chair. The cheery clipper worked on Spur's reddish-brown hair, snipping and talking incessantly about his eldest daughter—ripe for marriage.

Strange job he'd been handed, the Secret Service agent thought. The telegram from General Halleck in Washington was cryptic, as usual, but he got the gist. The growing town of Quintoch, Kansas, was living in fear. Three men had been hung in the last two weeks, all in or near their own homes. The county sheriff was stumped. No one witnessed the hangings and he had no suspects.

But there was one lead. All three men had been members of the Kansas 14th Regiment during the Civil War. They'd been recruited rather late and had taken part in the deep push into Georgia that finally led to the fall of Atlanta as well as the South.

That was the only thing the sheriff had been able to come up with. Sheriff Andrews had requested state aid but Kansas had in turn contacted the Secret Service in Washington. They, in turn, assigned Spur the job of finding the murderer.

"Pretty as a peach!"

Spur folded the telegram. "What?"

"Pretty as a peach, she is. Cooks good, too!" The barber lopped off one last hunk of hair.

He looked at his reflection in the misty mirror across from the chair. "I'm sure she is, Sam. Sure she is."

"You better hurry up and meet her or she'll marry someone else!"

"I thought you said she was nineteen," Spur said as he pulled the hair-strewn cloth from his chest.

"She is!" The barber sliced some soap into a mug, poured some water into it and whipped up the shaving cream. "She's just picky."

"Hmmmmm."

The barber honed the straight-edged razor on the strop. "Best thing of all—I taught her how to shave!"

An hour later Spur tipped his wide-brimmed hat at a pretty woman on the train as he sat beside her.

"Morning, ma'am," he said cheerily as he fit his six-foot two-inch frame into the cushioned seat.

"Don't you morning ma'am me!" The woman straightened her lace collar and glared at him. She looked to be about 35.

"Only trying to be friendly," he said.

"Try somewhere else!" She arched her eyebrows, emphasizing her ice-blue eyes. "I'm a human being, after all, not just a woman!"

"What?" Spur shook his head. "I must have missed something."

She frowned. "All you men are just the same. You treat us like we're delicate flowers, like we'll wilt if we don't hear kindly words. I ain't no flower, mister!"

Spur sighed and looked at the woman. A white lace and pearl trimmed dress covered her from her neck to the toes of her red boots, but it didn't take much imagination to see what was under all that cloth. "Right."

"You treat us like queens and expect us to be happy with that."

"And why not?" Spur settled in on the bench. This was going to be a long trip.

She turned to him, eyes flaring. "We want more than that. The women of the United States are tired! Sick and tired of it! We want the right to vote! We want the same rights as men enjoy in this great country of ours!" She panted. "And we'll get them! Don't fool yourself about that! We'll get what we so richly deserve!"

Spur sighed. It had been a while since he'd met a suffragette.

CHAPTER TWO

Spur McCoy walked onto the train station in his city clothes. He collected his luggage and ambled into town. Quintoch was a growing city of 6,000, surrounded by rich farmlands and ranches, a once sleepy settlement that had blossomed since the Kansas-Pacific railroad had pushed through on its way west.

The streets were filled with buggies, wagons and riders. Fancy ladies lolled on the boardwalks in front of saloons, fanning their satin-draped bodies in an attempt to escape the heat. Cowboys and farmers bustled into the Quintoch County Bank. Hisses and metalic clanks issued from the two blacksmith shops that serviced the town. Horses of every color and description were lined up at the hitching posts.

Spur had assumed the role of a well-heeled businessman from back east and was wearing his best suit. He'd say he was looking for a place to start a business—any business, since he had so many and so much money. This story would work for him, allowing him to pierce the fabric of the town and discover the killer.

The Diamond Ridge Hotel (est. 1863) seemed an appropriate place for a man like him to stay. The three-story structure had just been whitewashed. Stain glass windows sparkled along its walls. It was indeed fine.

The lobby was roomy, filled with leather chairs, gleaming spittoons and transplanted easterners. He registered and went to his third floor room, dropped his luggage and headed for the sheriff's office.

A gaunt, kind-faced man looked up from his desk as Spur walked in.

"Sheriff Andrews?"

"That's right. Who might you be?" He rubbed the bald spot on the top of his head.

Spur looked around the office. They were alone, no deputies in sight. He might as well be up front with the man. "Spur McCoy. Washington sent me."

Andrews stood, smiled and extended his hand. "Sure am glad to see you, Mr. McCoy. I hadn't heard you were coming into town."

"Just got in on the train."

They shook hands.

"You know about my problem?"

"Yes. That's why I'm here."

"Have a seat." He gestured to the wooden chair in front of his desk. Jonathan Andrews frowned. "I can't figure out who's been doing it," he admitted. "Lots of folks are worried. Most of them are mad at me."

"But you figure it's the same man doing the

killing? That hung those three men?''

"Almost sure."

He opened a drawer and hauled out a hangman's noose. Frayed ends showed where it had been cut off a foot above the knot. "This here's the last one. Found it around Troy Benton's neck eight days ago. It was his wife who discovered him, hanging dead in his parlor."

Spur examined the knotted rope.

"If you'll notice—"

"It's different," Spur said, cutting off the sheriff's words. "Only twelve knots."

"Yep. The other two were just like it."

"So whoever killed Benton killed the others."

"'Pears so." Andrews sipped some tepid coffee. "I can't understand what kind of killer would hang a man in his own house. That's pretty risky."

"Maybe he wants to be caught. Stranger things have happened. Where was his wife?"

Andrews flushed. "She—ah—was out with the preacher's son that night. All night. Millie found him kicking the wind when she got back in the morning. She never has been the faithful kind. Known her since she was kneehigh to a cricket."

Spur nodded. He'd run into the type a few times himself. "So I'm looking for a man who's killed three men, using the same kind of noose. And all three were ex-soldiers from the Fourteenth Regiment."

"Yep. That's what started me to thinking. Since all those boys were down South during the war, maybe some Southerner's getting his revenge or something." Andrews shook his head.

"It isn't unheard of."

"Hell, I don't know. It's been rattling around my

brain for three weeks now. I been thinking about it for so long I'm going crazy. And last night I woke up and suddenly knew who it was!''

''Yeah? Who?''

The sheriff laughed. ''I was convinced it was Stafford the undertaker tryin' to get more work.''

Spur smiled. ''Any other connection between the three men besides their army careers?''

''Well, they used to drink at the Prairie King Saloon. Them and four others. All of them were recruited right here for the Fourteenth Regiment. Have their own tables near the back. Get together most every day, talking about the old times. That's how I knew that the dead men were ex-soldiers—they were always there with their friends.''

Spur nodded. ''No Southerners in town stirring up trouble lately? No men with obvious bad feelings about Yankees?''

''None that I've seen. And I've been lookin'. Ever'where.'' He gazed at Spur. ''I just don't get it. Hope you can. If any more men are hung the whole place'll go crazy. People'll start moving out. Hell, they might run me out of town!''

''I'll do my best, Andrews. And I'll be in touch.''

''Thanks, Mr. McCoy.'' He rose with Spur. ''You let me know if I can help you.''

''I will.''

Kay Fordham snuck into the hardware store, a smile playing on her delicious face. A young man in overalls was bent over, struggling with the locked lower door on a rifle cabinet. She padded up to him. Blue eyes sparkling with mischief, she swatted his big behind with her beaded purse.

Jack Hastings spun around, rage and confusion on his face. When he recognized Kay he grabbed her thin wrists. "Woman! You know I don't like that! Besides, what if my boss was around?"

Kay laughed throatily and wrestled away from him. "Old man Tompkins sleeps until noon. And anyway, I like it!"

"You—you—" Jack sighed. "What am I gonna do with a woman like you, Miss Fordham?"

"You know exactly what to do. And don't call me miss!" She lifted her left eyebrow and repositioned her white bonnet. "Come on, Jack. I haven't seen you for a week. Been out of town all that time—alone."

The youth turned his attention back to the case and chuckled. "Alone? I don't believe you. You're never alone. Unless you scared off all the men." He worked the lock. "Damn thing won't open! The key must be bent or something."

"Hey, Jack, I just got off the train and came here specially to see you!"

"So you saw me. I'm busy." He rattled the key, sending the wood and glass cabinet rocking back and forth. "Darn!"

"If that's how your gonna be, I'll leave!" she pouted.

"You believe in women's rights," Jack mumbled. "I believe in my rights. And right now I'm busy!"

"Fine! Just don't show up on my door some lonely night when you want some company—in bed!"

Kay swirled to the door, a vision in white silk and pearls.

Amos Tompkins held the door for her and tipped his hat. "Good afternoon, Kay!" he said cheerily.

She snarled. "I'm perfectly capable of opening it myself. And what's so good about it?"

The store owner sneered. "When you suffragettes gonna be satisfied?" he asked, watching her hips swaying back and forth.

Kay turned to him and yelled. "As soon as we figure out how to live without men!"

"Women!" Amos said as he made his way through the cluttered store to his clerk. "What's with that lady?" he asked. "How come she's more ornery than ever?"

Jack Hastings blew out his breath and stood. "Heck, boss, I don't know." He dusted his hands on the legs of his overalls. "She's just mad at me."

Amos crossed his arms. "Thought you two was getting on mighty fine. What'd ya do, take her arm while you was out strolling—or some other crime?"

Hastings grinned at the joke. "Course not! I'd never do nothing like that with her."

Truth was, Jack thought, he was starting to hate Kay—the Yankee with her high-falutin' ways, her double-talk about female *this*, female *that*. Why couldn't he find a nice Southern gal?

"I'll let you get to your work, son," Amos said, and reached toward a stack of tools. "These the new hammers?"

Jack glanced over at him. "No. They came in last month. Remember?"

"Oh, sure, sure."

The aged man set the hammer down. Hastings stared at it for five minutes after Amos left. He felt that old ache in his head again.

* * *

It could even be one of them, Spur thought as he watched four men splashing whiskey into glasses and playing cards. The informal 14th Regiment club was in session in the back of the Prairie King Saloon.

Maybe one of the ex-soldiers had a grudge against them. Maybe he was killing them one at a time. It could have something to do with the war, something that had eaten away at his mind until he'd gone crazy.

Spur settled back into his chair and surveyed the loud, smoke-filled, dusty saloon, thinking.

Say one of the Kansas regiment found out he didn't have the guts to do the job during the war. Maybe he'd disgraced his friends and had suffered through their disgust and anger. They'd forgotten all about it but he never had, and was working to kill off the old pain. It was a possibility.

The four men seated around the table near the stairs were cut from the same cloth. Unshaven, long-haired, tired-eyed souls who seemed to be drifting through life. They drank without stopping, argued at the end of card games, whistled at the plain-faced whores and spat on the floor.

Maybe they'd gone downhill faster since their friends started dying. Maybe they were running scared, thinking they were next. Maybe—

''Hello, East.''

He looked up. An almost-attractive girl in a green dress that matched her eyes leaned over Spur's table, staring at him. Most of her chest spilled out from the low neckline.

''Hello yourself. Why call me East?''

The fancy lady smiled. "With a suit like that you gotta be from the East!" She fluttered her eyelashes. "Buy a girl a drink?"

"Sorry, no. I got some thinking to do."

"You can think with me!" She widened her smile, showing broken teeth.

"I have to be sitting down to use my brain."

She sighed. "Okay! But it's on your head! You're condemning me to a longer sentence in this hell-hole!" She wandered off and approached another man.

Spur turned back to the four men. Who was it?

CHAPTER THREE

"I loved my husband, don't misunderstand me," Millie Benton said as she looked out the lace-rimmed curtains. "He was good to me. Though he played cards and drank too much, he never hit me or nothing like that. But he—he was—"

Spur stood in the widow's parlor. "Look, Mrs. Benton, if you'd rather not talk about it, I'll understand."

The blonde woman touched her high cheekbones, smearing a spot of rouge. "I'll be frank with you, Mr. McCoy. Troy was boring." She poured a glass of sherry and sipped it. "All he ever talked about was the war. He'd go on and on about it, from the time he got up in the morning until he went to work at the telegraph office. When he came home it was the same thing all over again. That went on for years. Finally, he started hanging around the Prairie King so much he was practically living over there." She frowned. "So I found other friends—male friends, if you get my meaning."

Spur nodded. "Got it."

"When I walked in that morning I couldn't believe my eyes. I hadn't slept more than a few hours so I wasn't sure I was seeing straight. But there he was—my Troy hanging from that beam right there, dead as the frog I found in the garden yesterday morning." Millie's face went white. She drained the glass and set it down. "I'm sorry. I just can't help you. That's all I know."

"I appreciate the information, Mrs. Benton."

"You—you gonna catch the man who did it?"

"Yes."

Millie bit her lower lip. "I may not have been the best wife, or Troy the best husband, but we loved each other. We really did!" Tears brimmed in her eyes.

He patted her back and walked to the door. "I'm sure you did."

An hour later Spur was digging into a thick slab of roast beef. The juicy meat was expertly cooked, and the other guests at the hotel dining table raved over their meal.

As he was piling more boiled potatoes and carrots on his plate a woman sat next to him. He turned to greet her and nearly dropped his fork. It was the suffragette from the train.

"Why hello again!" she said sweetly, nodding to Spur as she spread the napkin on her lap.

Spur had to admit she was an attractive woman, despite what came out of her mouth. "Hello yourself!" He stuffed a hunk of carrot into his mouth and chewed.

"I'm sorry I was so rude on the train earlier today," Kay Fordham said. "I was just nervous, I guess. I hate those iron horses. Every time I'm on them I know the whole train's gonna fly off the tracks and kill me.''

He swallowed and looked blankly at her.

"So do you accept my apology?''

"Sure.'' Another carrot.

"I'm Kay Fordham.'' She stuck out her hand.

Spur laughed and shook it. "Spur McCoy. You know, you're bound to get into trouble spreading around your ideas.''

"Don't I know it! Half the men in this town think I'm plum crazy.''

"More than half!'' a bearded man said from the end of the table.

Kay ignored him. "Half the women, too!''

She stabbed two slices of beef and transferred them to her plate from the serving dish. "But some of them think I'm right. A few of us women get together every Saturday morning to talk, figure out what to do.''

"Oh.'' A potato this time, drenched in melted butter. It was ambrosia, Spur thought.

Kay took off her bonnet and hung it on the back of the chair, revealing a mound of bright red hair. "I hate those things! So frilly and uncomfortable. They keep the sun off my face but there's no reason to wear them inside.'' She looked accusingly at the four other female diners who kept on eating, hats tied around their chins.

"What're you doing here tonight, Miss Fordham?'' the bearded man asked. "Decided to eat some good cookin' rather than your slop?''

A white-haired woman cuffed the aged man's shoulder.

"It's true,'' Kay said, glancing at Spur. "I can do

lots of things better than cooking." Her blue eyes were warm and inviting.

"I'm sure you can, Miss Fordham. I'm sure you can."

After dinner the suffragette tagged along with Spur.

"Do you wanna?" she asked.

"Wanna do what?" Spur said it, though he knew darn well what she meant.

"You know—that!"

He laughed and considered it. She sure was a good-looking woman. "Sure. Of course!" he said. "But Kay, it's two hours till dark!"

"Well, we might be able to finish by then. Let's go!" She grabbed his hand and pulled him along the boardwalk.

Spur laughed. He wasn't about to say no to a woman like her.

Kay's house was austere and spotlessly clean, but Spur barely saw it as the wild woman whisked him to the bedroom. There was something so arousing about her, he thought as she stood panting before him, her chest heaving, eyes wild with desire as she yanked off her hated bonnet and unpinned her hair.

She might have been fighting for women's rights, but at the moment she was all woman. Spur kicked off his boots and removed his holster.

They stood before each other, staring, bodies tense, breath blasting from their lips. The man and woman almost dared each other to start.

Spur touched the neckline of her beautiful satin dress.

"Do it! Rip it! Tear my dress off, Spur!"

"Sure you're not having second thoughts—" he started.

"Damn you!"

He grabbed the material and tore it.

"Oh!"

Another rip.

"Yes!" she gasped.

He cleaved the bodice in half. Spur smiled in delight and surprise at her bare breasts. None of those fancy female underthings for this woman. Under the dress she was as naked as the day she was born.

Kay arched her back and sighed as Spur denuded her. Pearls and shiny threads rained down to the carpet. He unwrapped her like a package until she was completely naked.

The sharp-tongued woman's body glowed in the diffused sunlight. Spur felt the pressure build in his crotch. His eyes misted as he stared at the red patch between her legs.

"Are you here to do it or just to look?" Kay demanded. She grabbed his groin and squeezed it. "Get that thing out and use it!"

"Yes ma'am—I mean—ah!" He fumbled over the words as he took off his pants. "Yes, Kay!"

Stripped from the waist down, he grabbed the woman's shoulders and threw her onto the bed. She sighed as their bodies slapped together, as she took the full weight of the man.

"Oh heck, honey! Let me up there on top!"

Spur looked at her. "Huh?"

Kay squirmed. "Come on." She pushed him off her, rolled him onto his back and knelt over his crotch. "It feels just as good," she said.

"Okay."

Spur wasn't one to argue with a lady—even those who didn't think they were ladies. Her white breasts wiggled erotically as she lined up their bodies.

"This is gonna feel soooo good," Kay said, grunting. Finally in the proper position, the woman lowered her hips, impaling herself on Spur.

"Christ!" he hissed as he entered her.

"Leave him outa this!"

Lower, lower. Hot, wet sensations flooded through him. Kay shivered and threw her head from side to side. He watched his penis disappear into the woman's red pubic hair. The feelings grew more and more intense as she took him inch by inch.

"Spur, honey, I never thought it'd take this long!" Kay said. She panted as she slowly sank down.

"You complainin'?" he asked, gently pinching her nipples until they grew into hard, pink lumps.

"No. Never!"

Kay's round bottom finally pressed against his thighs. Spur grunted at the full penetration, at the erotic heat of her body. He lowered his hands to her hips and grabbed the soft cheeks. "This is kinda fun!" he said. "I mean, doing it this way."

"I know. Why'd you think I wanted it? Some of us women have good ideas, too." She pushed harder onto him for emphasis.

"Why Kay Fordham! How you do talk!" Spur said, reveling in their intimate connection.

She exploded into action, pulling up and slamming down onto him. Spur grunted as she hit home and bucked like a wild horse, hair flying, breasts bouncing, gasps blasting out of her lips as she pleasured herself.

He grasped her buttocks and guided her harder onto his erection. "Yeah, do it, woman!" he said. "Show me what you can do!"

"Oh, Spur!"

The bodies banged together at the hips, slick flesh slapping against wet skin. Spur stared at the woman who worked him over, at her lovely face radiating sexual bliss, her red lips and wide eyes, at the red mane of hair that flew around her head.

"Yes! Yes! Yes!" she chanted on each downward thrust.

Her cries intensified. Kay grabbed her breasts and squeezed them. She threw back her head and strangled out a scream, ramming harder onto him, shaking and shivering through an orgasm.

"Oh yes, Kay. Yes!"

His thighs tightened. Every nerve in his body strained for release. Spur bent his knees, lifted the sighing woman and jabbed up into her with powerful thrusts, pushing into her liquid opening.

"Give it to me. Give it to me!" she gasped.

He grunted and pistoned into her. The brass bed squeaked beneath them. The room blacked out. Spur drove home and ejaculated, gritting his teeth. He banged his head against the down pillow in time with each powerful spurt.

Spur drove into her ten times and fell back on the bed, exhausted, drained. Kay flopped onto him and kissed his neck. Their slick bodies melted together as they panted and held each other. McCoy closed his eyes and smelled the woman's hair, nuzzled it, kissed her ear and sighed as she continued to spasm around his shrinking penis.

Groggy, Spur pried apart his right eyelid. Diffused sunlight splattered the room. Kay smiled when he looked at her. They kissed, lightly touching lips.

"That was heaven."

"It certainly was." She moved off him but pressed her body against his.

"Who would have thought this would happen when we met on the train?"

Kay smiled. "I would. In fact, I did. I'm just sorry I opened my big mouth."

"No harm done." Spur luxuriated in the tremendous peace that oozed through him.

The bedroom door burst open. "Kay, dear, I know I'm late, but—"

They turned and looked at the horrified woman standing in the bedroom door.

"Oh, hi, Mrs. Germer." Kay's voice was sweet.

The middle-aged woman blushed and held her purse with both hands, mouth open, eyes wide, at the sight of their nude bodies.

"Oh, our meeting! I'm sorry," Kay said. "I guess I kind of forgot all about it." She smooched Spur's cheek. "I've been busy with Mr. McCoy here."

Spur laughed. They'd been caught so he might as well make the best of it. "Afternoon, Mrs. Germer." Spur smiled at her. Nothing could bother him now.

"Good afternoon!" Her gaze dipped below his waist. "A real pleasure meeting you!"

"I hope you're not shocked," Kay said. "After all, this is what we women have to fight for. The right to do anything we want, whenever we want. Right?''

''Why, of course. Of course, Kay! I'm not shocked. Maybe surprised, but not shocked. In fact, it's been a delight, Kay, Mr. McCoy.'' She nodded.

''If you wouldn't mind waiting in the parlor I'll be out soon.''

''Fine, Kay. Take your time. And if I was ten years younger I'd take your place!'' She cackled and walked off.

The door closed. Spur laughed with Kay as they jumped up and dressed.

''That's one of my most promising members,'' she said, selecting a new dress to replace the one that lay ribboned on the ground.

''Great. Just don't promise me to her.'' He pulled on his pants.

CHAPTER FOUR

Jack Hastings wiped his hands on his overalls. The air in the hardware store hung like a thick curtain. It smothered him. He couldn't breathe.

To make things worse, they hadn't had more than two customers that afternoon. Amos Tompkins had told him if business didn't pick up he might have to fire him.

Hastings closed his eyes and felt the flames of fire licking the back of his head. The pain grew more intense so he looked around the store, desperately searching for something to make him forget the awful throbbing in his skull.

The brass bell on the door, the one that Mr. Tompkins said had come all the way from India, clanged. Jack Hastings looked up from behind the counter and smiled.

"Hello," the vivacious, smiling woman said as she closed her parasol with white-gloved hands. "I hope you can help me. I need a pitcher and basin."

"We have a wide selection, miss," Jack said.

She waved the parasol. "Not just any pitcher and

basin—a proper one. White English ceramic with red roses and a hummingbird.'' The thin-waisted, pretty girl seemed firm on that point.

''Hmmmm.'' He stepped to the shelf behind him. ''Why that particular design?''

She lowered her eyes. ''It reminds me of home.''

He heard it then—the slightest hint of an accent. A southern girl! Jack fought off his excitement and scanned the gleaming sets that he dusted off every morning.

''How about this one?'' he turned to her and pointed at it.

She sighed. ''No, that's not quite right. It has to be perfect.''

''You from Georgia?'' he asked, continuing to hunt.

''That's right. How'd you know?''

''So'm I. Just outside of Atlanta.'' He grasped a ewer and handed it to her. ''This one should do it, ma'am.''

She regarded it and held out her hands. Jack tenderly deposited the ceramic pitcher on her gloves, gazing eagerly at her.

''Well, it'll do. I know I'll never see the other one again. It's been gone these ten years.''

''Yes, ma'am. Lots of us lost things in the—the—'' Steely knives stabbed into his brain.

''Please, don't remind me.'' She shivered under her yellow bonnet. ''How much you asking for this?''

''Ah, dollar-fifty.''

She placed it on the counter and opened her purse. ''Wrap it up, please, sir.''

He grinned at her voice, the accent was coming

through. Visions washed through his mind—the scent of magnolias in the cool evening air, tree-lined drives, the young women in their hoop skirts, the smell of frying chicken, his father, his mother. . . .

Jack's hands were shaking by the time he'd fastened paper around the pair of utensils. He took the woman's money and deposited it in the cash drawer.

"Thank you kindly, sir." She nodded to him and reached for the package.

"Wait!" he said. "Uh, is there anything else I can interest you in?"

"I'm sorry. I must be leaving."

"But—but—" He grabbed the paper-wrapped ceramics and looked at the floor. "Sorry to bother you, miss, but it's been so long since I talked to a pretty girl from home," Jack grabbed his scalp and rubbed it.

"Well, ah, I really have to be going." The southern woman couldn't quite remove the package from his fingers.

Hastings glanced up at her. "Please!"

Her cheeks colored. "Sir, my husband is waitin'!"

"Alright, take it!"

The confused woman wrenched them from his hands and swirled away. "Good day!"

Jack slammed his fist onto the counter as the Indian bell tinkled and the woman left. Her husband. Probably some Yankee who'd robbed her parents blind, who'd gotten fat off the wealth of the South during the war.

Heck, he hadn't wanted to get into her bloomers.

All he wanted to do was talk to her. But she was
just like all the rest—afraid to remember what had
happened, afraid to relive the horrors of those last
days before their world crumbled to dust, stomped
under the boots of Northern soldiers.

Jack Hastings pounded his neck with his fists.
He remembered all right. He was 11 on his
parents' plantation. There was a squirrel in the
pecan tree beside the cookhouse. He'd shinneyed
up the trunk, innocently hunting when it
happened.

It happened!

The memories seared his brain. He slumped over
the counter. The muscled young man choked back
a cry.

"I keep telling you, I'm not from the east," Spur
McCoy said to the green-wrapped saloon girl.

"Oh, sure. Look, everyone out here's whatever
they wanna be. I mean, look at me!" Gussie
Granger guffawed and spilled some watered
whiskey down her throat.

Spur was too busy looking at something else—at
the demoralized men that constituted the local
remnants of the 14th Regiment. They seemed
darker than ever as they went through the motions
of playing cards.

"You know, I didn't always do this," Gussie
said, breaking his concentration. "I used to be a
nice city girl in Philadelphia. Engaged and everything."

He glanced at her.

"Then that ape dumped me. I didn't know what
to do! But this man said he'd pay my way out here

if I'd be willing to work for him. Never said what I'd be doing, you unnerstand, though I had a hunch." She laughed. "So I've been here six months, still working for him, not earning a dime. He takes all the money and I do all the work!"

"I'm sorry, Gussie, but I really don't have—"

"Sure, you're sorry!" she said, cutting off his words. "Meanwhile I'm breaking my back trying to earn enough money so I can get outa this dump!" She crossed her legs and swung her leg up and down in front of him. "That real short guy over there at the bar's my boss. I still owe him a hundred bucks. Then I'll leave." She grasped his arm. "Hey, how about it?" Gussie's eyes were red with alcohol. "You know? Help a poor kid get back home?"

Spur sighed and shook his head. "I'm sorry, Gussie. I have this rule."

She retracted her hand and stood. "I know—you don't pay for it." The fancy lady straightened her bodice and forced a smile. "Wish me luck?"

"You have it."

Gussie slouched over to the back table near the stairs. "Come on, Sam," she said to one of the ex-soldiers, a beefy man with a thick brown moustache. "It's about time you saw me again. Ain't it?"

"Hell! I'm right in the middle of a game!" He hesitated and threw down his cards. "I guess so."

The angel of mercy winked at Spur as she took the man up to her room.

The remaining three men started talking. Spur moved to a closer table to pick up their voices.

"Least he's having a good time," a gaunt-faced

man said.

"He's trying, Les. I don't know about you boys, but I'm running scared."

"Hell, Hughes," Les said. "You wasn't never scared during the War!"

"Damn straight! But this ain't the war." Mike Hughes' left eyelid twitched as he stared at his hand. "We can't see the enemy. We don't even know who the hell it is!"

The men fidgeted in their chairs, laying down and picking up cards.

"Pure coincidence," Lester Fields finally said. "That's all it is."

"Bullshit!" a third ex-soldier said.

"Right!" Hughes patted his shoulder. "That's all it is. I—I hope."

Jack Hastings walked into the crowded Prairie King Saloon. He ordered a whiskey from the one-armed barback and gulped it down, staring at a group of men near the back of the big, smoky room. The fiery alcohol seemed to increase the pain in his head. Soon, he thought. Soon it'd be gone again.

He slapped a dollar on the bar and took the bottle. As he drank and watched the men, Jack drifted back in time, to the glorious days of his youth.

Jack remembered the plantation best—a huge, white collonaded structure. His boyhood had been as happy as it could be, growing up surrounded by money and power. His father had his hand in every aspect of Atlantan life. He called on the mayor whenever he had a problem. He owned five blocks of prime downtown property.

Life on Pecan Knoll was peaceful. Even after the Civil War had started it continued on much as it had been. His father fought for a few months before coming back home, wounded and readying to die. But he'd recovered and soon was back ordering the servants around.

At 11, Jack Hastings had been far too young to join up, and his father absolutely forbade him from pretending to be older to get into the army. He wanted him safe and sound at home. The Hastings had done their part to fight off the Yankees.

Jack closed his eyes and let his chin drop to his chest. That part was easy to remember. What came next was excruciating, but he remembered it. He had to.

The pecan tree seemed gigantic. Wearing a mended pair of pants, Jack had climbed up it, slingshot stuck into his back pocket, following a squirrel who was after the nuts. The scent of ten pecan pies cooling in the cookhouse window drifted through the air.

Sunlight blinded his eyes as he moved up the big old branch. The squirrel, alarmed at his intrusion, bolted up into a mass of emerald leaves.

"Come here, you ole critter," Jack had said. He stalked it as quietly as he could but soon lost it. "Darn you!"

He looked around. His parents weren't in sight. They'd warned him about climbing the tree but he just couldn't resist inching farther into its leafy heights. The branch slanted up, higher and higher from the ground.

He pushed into the tangled twigs and leaves.

Unripe pecans hung like jewels around his ears. He was fully meshed in the tree's fruitfulness.

He heard his father yelling somewhere far underneath but the squirrel was too tantalizing to back down now. He'd face his father later. Now—

Rifles cracked. Horses pounded the ground. The tree shook with the fury of their hooves. The squirrel popped into view, nibbling on a nut. More shooting, more shouts, more full-throated screams.

It was too much to ignore. Jack started down the branch, listening to the growing confusion. It was worse than anything he had ever heard. The smell of gunpowder drifted up into the tree, stinging his nose, giving him a headache.

Jack stopped and looked at the ground. Men. Lots of men in uniforms. He didn't recognize the blue suits at first. Then he knew.

Yankees! There, on his father's plantation.

His 11-year-old mind raced. Should he go down? Try to help? No. His father had told him what they do. They killed innocent children and women. They were ruthless, merciless monsters.

He hugged the branch, shut his eyes and tried to melt into the tree. Jack gasped as the squirrel hopped down his back on some kind of mission.

The sounds of the clash below him grew more intense. He heard his father yelling, then his mother.

No. Not his mother. God no!

Acrid smoke filtered through the leaves. Cannons blasted. Rifles discharged. Jack didn't know how long he laid there, hidden in the glorious pecan, immobilized with fear.

He heard loud popping sounds. Jack pried his

bark-imprinted cheek from the wood and looked out. The house was on fire, the huge white columns cracking and buckling, sending the upper porch crashing to the ground.

The bluebellies had left. They'd burned his house. But where was his mother, his father?

The little boy watched his home flare up into a spectacular blaze, unwilling to climb down the tree, afraid of what he might find there.

Finally, Jack couldn't wait any longer. He slipped down the branch, down the trunk. He huffed as his small feet slapped against the ground. Then he turned around.

He barely saw the 50-foot flames reaching for heaven, or the dead plantation workers and servants littering the ground, the broken rifles and bleeding, broken soldiers.

All his young eyes could take in were the two motionless figures sprawled near the front porch. His mother, her dress and underthings ripped off, her legs wide apart.

His father, a bayonet in his chest, blood soaked through his white shirt and white coat.

Dead. Both of them dead.

The scene telescoped. Jack Hastings started to shake as he stood there, staring at them, the air thick with the stench of death. His knees buckled and his eyes blurred.

The whole building trembled. He looked up as the second story fell, splintering into a black and white mosaic of destruction.

The innocent boy turned and ran into the pecan trees, stumbling over roots, crying as he realized what had happened. And his head pounded!

Jack Hastings opened his eyes. The saloon was emptying out, the fancy ladies were either busy or had gone to sleep now that their customers were leaving. He took one last drink from the glass and set it on the bar.

He stole a look toward the stairs. Just one man sat there—the one that looked thinner than a starved goat. Jack rubbed his neck, trying to massage away the agony, planning.

He needed rope. He needed the hammer.

He needed both things to clear his head.

CHAPTER FIVE

It's well past midnight, Spur thought as he sat hunched in his chair. Business in the Prairie King Saloon was slowly winding down. Spur got up and followed as the two ex-members of the Kansas 14th Regiment stumbled from the bar, out into the cool night air. They yelled goodbyes and wandered off in different directions.

He knew that all the hangings had occurred at night, so he'd decided to follow the men home, watching for any signs of trouble. He could follow one of them home at least. He chose Hughes, the one who'd admitted he was worried about the killings.

An owl circled overhead, flashing across the moon as Spur walked behind the man. Though Hughes might be drunk and afraid, his steps were sure, measured, as he automatically returned home, a task he must have done hundreds of times since the end of the war.

Hughes went down Mahoney Street and eventually disappeared into one of the small homes on the tree-lined avenue. Spur grunted. He should be safe enough.

McCoy returned to Main Street but the other man wasn't in sight. He checked the surrounding streets and, finding nothing, assumed he would also be safe in bed before too long. The Secret Service agent went to his hotel for a good night's sleep.

"Need some help?"

Lester Fields grunted. "Sure. My feet don't seem to work right," he said, slurring his words.

The stranger wrapped his arm around Fields' shoulders and gripped his ribs to prevent him from falling face-first into the dusty side street.

"Don't know what's wrong with 'em," Fields said.

"Seems like you had a few too many."

"Is that a fact? Maybe." Lester turned to look at his benefactor. "You sure seem familiar. Ain't I seen you somewhere around town?"

The man smiled. "Probably. I work in town. Jeez, you are drunk, sir!"

Fields laughed. "Yeah! And I don't care who knows it!" he yelled.

"Keep your voice down," he said gently. "You wouldn't want to wake up the ladies in town, would you?"

"Sure. But not with my voice."

Both men chuckled as they slowly progressed down the street.

"Now where'd my house go?" Lester Fields said, eyes rolling as he surveyed the darkened buildings. "I know it's around here somewhere." He stopped.

"Is it that one?"

"Nope."

"How about that one?"

"Uh-uh. Ah! There it is!"

"Good. Now let's get you home."

"Alright. And thanks." Fields pushed toward it, guided by the other man's strong hands. "You're a real pal, you know that?" he said, looking at him through bloodshot eyes.

"Yes," Jack Hastings said.

The light blinded him.

"Hughes!" the sheriff thundered. "You know what the hell time it is?"

"Yes, sir."

"It's a mite late to come courting my Annabelle!"

"Sorry, Sheriff Andrews," Mike Hughes said as he stood on the man's porch. "Fact is, I ain't here to do that."

He stared at the red-faced, sleepy-eyed man who held the kerosene lamp up to his face. "You see, I got this funny feeling."

Andrews snorted. "Hell! You should've taken care of that with Gussie or one of them other whores! Don't come here expecting Annabelle to take care of that. I still can't talk her into seeing you!"

"No, no, not *that* kinda feeling." Hughes wiped his sweating forehead. "Sheriff, I went home and took off my boots and—and I got—hell, I got scared like." He screwed up his face. "I don't know. I think somethin' bad's gonna happen."

The sheriff lowered the oil lamp. "Something

bad, huh? Something bad's gonna happen to you if you don't let me get my sleep!''

"But sheriff!''

Andrews sighed. "I know it's been hard on you lately, since your friends all started getting themselves killed!''

Hughes flinched.

"And it's only nat'rul that it'd start playing tricks in your head. But you gotta take it, boy! Hell, we were both in the war.'' He leaned closer. "We both know what it's like out there, facing the enemy. Never know when you might get it.''

"That's just fine, Sheriff Andrews! There ain't no enemy to face!'' He lowered his head in shame. "And it's eatin' away at me.''

Andrews slapped his left arm. "Come on, Hughes. Don't worry about it. If something's gonna happen, it happens. Besides, I got me some help. Just came in today. He's gonna find the murderin' bastard!''

"Really?''

"Sure as shit. Now git back to sleep. Think about anything else—even Annabelle, that hot-blooded daughter of mine. Talk to me in the morning. Okay?''

Hughes nodded. "Okay, sheriff.''

The door closed. He stood alone on the porch. Mike Hughes turned to face the street.

Now all he had to do was get home.

"Whew! I wouldn't have made it without you,'' Lester Fields said as he fell into a rail backed chair in his two room house. "Say, you wanna drink?''

"Sure.''

"Bottle's over there."

Jack Hastings poured them both a healthy slug. His headache was getting so bad he could barely see the glasses well enough to splash the whiskey into them. The tattoo beating in his brain flooded red mists in his vision. He managed it and handed the drink to Fields.

"Thank ye kindly!"

They drank.

As the fiery whiskey poured down his throat, Jack saw his mother lying in front of the plantation house. He saw her lifeless eyes staring at the sky, her wide-spread legs, the wounds.

Hastings looked at the drunken ex-soldier. He'd done it. He was the one. He'd killed them! Now if he could kill him, his headache would go away. He reached into his back pocket and held the long, cold object behind him.

"Hey, Fields, I got something for you."

"Yeah? What?" the drunkard asked, smacking his lips after draining the glass. "Another drink?"

"Nope."

Hastings grunted and brought it down. Hard metal crashed against bone. Fields slumped in the chair. Jack replaced the hammer, ran outside and searched for the coiled rope he'd hidden in the azaleas earlier that evening. Suddenly he was back in Georgia in his mind, but it was different this time. Everything was different.

He didn't stay in that pecan tree, shivering like the little boy he was. No. He jumped down into the noise and confusion, at the bluebellies running around, killing and burning everything he'd ever known. He was too small to be noticed, too young to be of any interest to the rampaging northerners.

Hastings saw himself picking up his father's new hammer and knocking them out as they ran past, one after another after another. He conked them all on their heads.

Then he got the rope and hung them, one by one, using that strange knot the cook's husband had taught him. He hauled them up around that old pecan tree branch where he'd hid and killed them.

Jack Hastings panted as he made the noose. He stared down at the groaning man. Doubt clouded his brain but he quieted it. This wasn't killing. It's never killing during a war. It's doing a job that has to be done, and this was a war.

"You killed them," Hastings said as he knelt and slipped the noose around Field's neck. "You killed my parents! You raped my mother! You didn't think anybody was left but I saw it. I saw it all!"

He pulled the rope tight. Fields coughed and opened his eyes. "What—what—"

Hastings smiled. "You're getting what you deserve, Yankee!"

Lester Fields' voice was scratchy. "You're the one! You've been killing my friends!"

He laughed. "Yeah. And you're gonna join 'em in hell!" Jack yanked on the rope, causing Fields to cough and gag on the floor.

The drunken man clawed at the smooth wood below him, rose to his knees and then grabbed the noose. Hastings tightened it, staring down at him, nostrils flaring, forehead sweating as he watched the man struggle.

"You're already dead, Fields!" he whispered. "I hung you ten years ago. You've been a ghost a-haunting me all these years. That's gonna change!''

Smiling, he looked up at the open beam that crossed the man's parlor. It was solid oak, six inches thick. It should take the weight, should work to wring every ounce of life from the killer.

Fields stumbled to his feet. Hastings pulled harder, enjoying the sight of the coiled rope squeezing the man's neck. Lester crashed to the ground. Red skin bulged out around the rope. He yelled and passed out.

Hastings frowned as the man lay motionless. That wasn't the way it was supposed to be. He grabbed the bottle and poured whiskey on Lester's face. The man sputtered, wheezed and lay still again.

Furious at the change of events, Jack Hastings moved to him and stood on the burly man's chest. He grabbed the rope with both hands and pulled it upward.

Hard. Harder. He strained his shoulder muscles as the thick neck resisted his pressure, as his feet held down the man's torso with his weight. He let go; Field's head banged down. He pulled and released, pulled and released, working out ten years of guilt, a decade of agonized frustration and torture.

Fields' eyes bulged out. His tongue emerged from his mouth and gruesomely lolled over his lower lip. The tortured rise and fall beneath Jack's feet halted.

Hastings stepped off the man's chest and dropped the rope. Was he? He felt the man's wrist. Yes. He was dead. Probably died of fright. The noose hadn't done it.

At least he'd accomplished his mission. He'd set out to do what he had to do. Now it was over. His head cleared, the red veils lifted from before his eyes as if they'd been whipped away in a breeze.

Lester Fields was dead.

Jack found a knife on the table and sliced the noose from the end of the rope. Now, what to do with the body? He didn't want the other Yankees to find this one so fast. Let them wait, Hastings thought. Let them think they're safe.

Where could he put it? He mused for a minute and then smiled.

Yes, it would be perfect.

Mike Hughes sat on his hard bed. He was exhausted but he couldn't shake off the feeling. Something was wrong.

Twice he rose to his feet and started toward the door, but both times he fell back onto the pigeon-feather mattress. Sheriff Andrews was right, Hughes told himself. There wasn't anything he could do. He was just letting it get to his head.

Go to sleep! He stretched out and closed his eyes, too tired to even take off his boots. But sleep wouldn't come. He tossed from side to side, finally settled in and dozed.

Annabelle Andrews, the sheriff's blonde haired daughter, walked along a sunny trail. She turned, looked to him and laughed. In his dream Mike Hughes hurried after her but she disappeared behind a bend.

When he saw her again Annabelle was dancing joyously among wildflowers. All around her his friends from the army swung from ropes in a stiff wind.

A storm moved in. Hughes felt a hand on his shoulder. He turned around.

"Ain't no time to come courting Annabelle," Sheriff Andrews said. "She's busy killing all your friends. Don't she look pretty up there?" he asked, proud of his progeny.

Hughes woke up screaming.

CHAPTER SIX

Knock. Knock. Knock.

Spur raised his head from the pillow. Who the hell was waking him up this early in the morning?

He glanced out the window. It was barely dawn. Yawning and rubbing his eyes, he answered the insistent, nerve-shattering pounding.

"Yeah?"

"Mister, Sheriff Andrews says you have to come quick!" a red-cheeked young man blurted. "Found another dead man. He's been hung!"

"Great," Spur said.

"The sheriff wants you there right now!"

"Okay, okay. Where'd they find the body?"

"In the well, in the center of town. You can't miss it."

"I'm on my way."

The youth ran off. Spur dragged his wide brimmed brown hat onto his head and forced his legs to move. He was dead tired, unusual since he'd gotten so much sleep.

He woke up fast as soon as he left the hotel

lobby. The street was filled with men and women, shouting and running toward the stone-faced well. By the time he strode up to it Spur was sufficiently roused. He saw Sheriff Andrews standing beside the well, hands on his hips, staring down at something on the ground.

Spur McCoy pushed through the crowd. "You asked for me, Andrews?" he said, glancing down. A man lay sprawled at his feet.

"Yep." The sheriff snarled. "That's Lester Fields," Andrews said. "A friend of mine." His eyes were dark. "I played cards with him every once in a while."

The man's body was soaked, stripped to the waist, the noose plainly visible around his neck. Spur bent and counted the knots. Twelve.

"Who found him?" he asked, fingering the frayed end of the rope.

"You wouldn't know her. Kay Fordham. Seems she came out here this morning to draw some water for coffee, but the bucket wouldn't come up."

"Oh yes—Kay."

More Quintoch residents pushed and shoved against Spur and the sheriff in their early morning zeal to see the latest murder victim.

"She pulled and pulled. Something seemed to slip and it came up. Came up all right, with Lester's shirt wrapped around it." Andrews winced. "Some men who were passing by lowered Drake into the well and he brought up the body." Sheriff Andrews wiped his sweaty forehead. "I don't like this, McCoy. Not one damn bit!"

"You and me both, Sheriff." Spur stood.

"It's funny. Mike Hughes came around my place late last night. He said he had a feeling something like this was gonna happen."

"He was right. Looks like the same killer as before. Same knotwork. But he left the others where he'd hung them, in their houses. Why dump this one here?"

"Hell if I know, McCoy." He sighed. "I better get Stafford to take him away and put him in a box. Whoever's been doing this sure has been giving the undertaker more work."

A weary eyed, scrawny man burst through the crowd. He looked down at the dead man, pulled off his hat and stared. His lower lip trembled.

"Fields," he said. "It's Fields!" He lunged for the sheriff. "I tole you! I tole you last night but you didn't listen to me!" He grabbed Andrews' shoulders and roughly shook him.

"Hey, calm down," Spur said, wringing the man off the sheriff.

"Stay outa this, stranger!" Hughes said. "This ain't your business!"

"The hell it ain't!" Andrews said. "Go home, Mike. It's too late to do anything about him now."

"But you—you could have—" the man blubbered.

The sheriff shook his head. "Buy you a cup of coffee?" he said to Hughes.

The man looked at him, mumbled and walked off.

"I better get the undertaker. Stay here and see that things stay calm."

"Sure, sheriff." Spur nodded.

" 'Bye, father!"

Spur turned and saw a woman standing next to him. She was a gorgeous, well-rounded beauty in a light blue dress powdered over with yards of lace and ribbons. She wasn't wearing a bonnet, so blonde curls cascaded from her head past her shoulders.

The young woman looked at Spur and then at the body. Her smiled faded. "That's—that's—Lester Hughes!" she exclaimed.

Spur nodded.

"And he's—he's dead!"

She fainted. Spur caught her in his arms and easily lifted her. "Make room!" he said to the people surrounding the body. He carried her to the bench that fronted Tompkin's Hardware Store, sat on it, and propped her head in his lap.

McCoy fanned her lovely face, admiring the curve of her nose, her firm cheekbones, red lips and fluttering eyelashes. This morning was getting better, he thought, as he cradled her head on his legs.

The woman took a deep breath and opened her eyes.

"Are you all right?" Spur asked.

"I guess so. What happened?"

"You fainted."

"Did I?" She rolled her eyes. "I remember now. I saw Lester. How silly of me."

She started to rise. Spur gently pressed her back down.

"You better rest for a while. Looks like you had quite a shock."

"No, really, I'm fine. And that feels fine." She

rubbed her head against his crotch and happily hummed.

Spur laughed. "You sure look fine."

She bounced up and giggled. "I'm Annabelle Andrews. The sheriff's my father."

"I kind of gathered that. Does that mean Spur McCoy wasted his time rescuing you?"

Annabelle pressed her hand to his. "No. I—I really did faint. I just made sure I did it beside you."

"Why?"

"Why do you think, silly? I wanted to meet you. My father told me all about you last night."

He'd been trapped, but it was a kind of trap he enjoyed. "I see."

Her sea-green eyes sparkled. "Anyway, we must have dinner," she said, poking at her hair. "Wouldn't that be fun? Just the two of us. I can cook anything you want—almost anything." She moved nearer to him, pressing her thigh against his. "You like chocolate cake?"

He nodded.

"Apple pie?"

"Uh-huh."

Annabelle leaned closer and put her lips against his right ear. "Me?"

The word tickled him.

"Yes!" He gasped as she bit his earlobe. "Boy, I sure am hungry!"

Annabelle laughed. "Then we've settled the menu. But it's too early to have dinner yet. What will we do with all this time?"

Spur looked at the old man carrying away

Lester Fields' body. First things first. "I have some business to take care of, but I'll see you later."

"I hope you're a man who keeps his word," Annabelle said, pouting.

"Always!" He kissed her cheek. As he started to rise Kay Fordham approached the bench where he sat with the woman.

"Spur McCoy," Kay said, her face blanched. "The sheriff said I should talk to you about this morning. But I don't know what I can tell you."

He stood. "I was just going to look for you."

"Is this business or pleasure?" Annabelle asked him, her words clipped.

"Business."

She rose. "Well, I guess I have to be going. Morning, Miss Fordham."

Kay nodded to her. "Morning, Andrews—uh, Annabelle."

She walked off.

"Should we sit?" Spur asked Kay.

"I'd rather stroll." The woman wrapped the white shawl closer around her shoulders as she walked, though the air was warming.

Spur thought about taking her arm and quickly realized the suffragette wouldn't like it. "You found him. Isn't that right?"

She nodded. "I'd gone to the well just like every other morning. And he was in it." She stared at the distant spire of the Quintoch Community Church.

"You didn't see anyone walking away from the well, did you?"

"No. No one. Not many people were up and around. It was just after five."

They were nearing the end of the boardwalk.

Kay's gaze was still fixed on the gleaming white steeple. Spur grabbed her arm and halted her.

"Don't you take—"

He pointed down at the drop off to the dusty street.

She shook her chin. "I'm sorry. Thought you were pulling one of those manly tricks on me."

"No—just tryin' to save your pretty neck, Kay." He released her arm and they continued on walking. Spur asked her questions until he'd run out of them.

She didn't know a thing.

The bodies wrestled, the man grunting, the woman moaning as they grappled and bucked together. The headboard banged into the wall, matching the tempo of his powerful thrusts.

"Harder. Harder!" she said.

He blindly drove into her, pinioning her willing body to the mattress, lavishing kisses on her face, neck and breasts as his scrotum slapped against her groin.

It threatened to happen too soon, too fast, so he slowed down, easing into a relaxed movement. The man rode up high, raising himself off her onto his fingers and toes, changing the angle of his penetration to give her more pleasure.

The woman convulsed, eyes shut, mouth open in an erotic circle of red flesh. She arched her back, lifting her breasts as their slick bodies slid together at the waist.

Pound. Slap. Thrust. Both groaned and held back for as long as they could, but soon the pressure was so intense they couldn't resist. The world dissolved

into a shimmering vacuum. He fell on top of her
and they shook and rattled through their mind-
bending orgasms.

Spur laid back on the mattress, panting. The
sheets stuck to his body.

"Are you surprised?" Annabelle asked as she
snuggled beside him.

"At what?" The ceiling still spun overhead,
whirling in his mind.

"That the sheriff's daughter has been so friendly
with you." She ran her fingers through his chest
hairs.

"Yeah, a little. I figured you'd be a hard prize to
catch, Annabelle Andrews!"

She softly laughed and pressed her ear to his
chest. "You mean, you figured you should have
climbed a greased pole to win me?"

"Something like that." He stroked her head.
"Lots of sheriffs wouldn't cotton to their daughters
doing what we just did."

"I can hear your heartbeat," she said. "So strong.
So fast inside there." Annabelle tapped his ribcage.
"My daddy isn't just any sheriff. Sure, he's trying
to find me a good husband, but he knows I'm not
about to wait around to have some fun. So he lets
me do what I want."

"That's very considerate of him. Almost
unbelievable." Spur was exhausted from their
morning exercises.

"Of course, I was wondering if I'd get the chance
to have any fun with you at all."

"What d'ya mean?"

"The way that Kay Fordham moved in on my
territory this morning. Everyone in town knows

that she's—well, she's worse'n me!'' Annabelle looked up at him.

Spur laughed, feeling his breathing returning to normal. "That was business, just like I told you. She found Lester Fields' body this morning. I had to question her about it. It's my job."

The young woman settled back down. "Okay. I believe you." She sighed. "Poor Lester. Daddy never did see anything in him—no future. He wouldn't even let the man in the house. And I think he really liked me. I don't know."

"I don't know much of anything right now." He sighed. "I feel like I just ran ten miles. You sure can wear me out, Annabelle."

She thumped his chest. "Don't blame it all on me, Spur McCoy. It does take two."

"Right."

Later, after they'd dressed, Spur answered a knock at his door. The same young man who'd awakened him that morning thrust a folded piece of paper at him.

"Here," he said, glancing into the room. "Telegram just came in for you. Mister Drake down at the telegraph office said you'd told him to let you know if one came in. Well, it did so I brung it to you."

Spur dug into his pocket. "Here you go."

The youth flipped the silver dollar. "Gee, thanks, mister. And hi there, Annabelle!" he yelled.

"Git outa here, kid!" she yelled, and threw a pillow at him.

Spur closed the door and returned to the bed. He opened the telegram and read it.

"What is it?" Annabelle asked, looking over his shoulder.

He lowered his brows. "Trouble."

CHAPTER SEVEN

The Kansas Pacific Railroad locomotive slowly pulled away from the Quintoch train station, puffing its way on west toward the real frontiers.

A fiftyish man turned aside as steam blasted at him from the train. "Remember now, Maddie, we're respectable like," the mustachioed well-dressed gent said. He struggled with the four carpetbags.

A black haired woman 30 years his junior hurried across the platform, boots clicking on the worn wood. "Oh, I remember all right, Vincent!" she said, dodging other new arrivals. "I remember everything you tell me, *daddy*. But does that mean we can't have any fun?"

"Of course not, Maddie. But slow down, will ya? My arms are about to fall off. I don't have all that young spirit that you've got!"

She smirked and increased her speed. "Serves you right for leaving me in the lurch back there!"

"You shut your mouth, child," he said to the unruly young woman. "I didn't leave you any-

61

where. And besides, you don't even know where you're going."

"I don't care. All I wanna do is feel the solid earth under my feet for a change. Four days on that damn train's enough to make anyone crazy!"

"Crazier, you mean!"

She jumped down the last two steps and pressed her pearl-buttoned boots to the dirt. "Ah! Real dirt! At last!" She untied her bonnet, threw it into the air and caught it, then lifted her billowing gray skirt and revealed her ankles.

Vincent Vandermeer dumped the carpetbags on the ground and brushed away her hands. "Land sakes!" he said. "Be reasonable, girl! Last thing we wanna do is attract undue attention." Vincent smiled to a frowning elderly couple as they walked past them.

"Oh, I know, Vince. But this last week's been hell! Ever since we done it."

He pointed his finger at her. "And none of that foul language, girl!"

Maddie Pryor sighed. "Alright."

"Just think of how much fun we're gonna have. Hey, girl, you're rich! You can do anything you want. Go anywhere, be anybody. Start a business. Buy a house. Little lady, you've got it all!"

She turned to him, brown eyes flashing in the Kansas sun. "Yeah. As long as you don't double-cross me."

Vincent stepped back. "Me? Don't let that thought into your pretty little head, Maddie!"

"You know, Vincent, sometimes you treat me like I really was your daughter!"

He grabbed her waist. "Someone has to keep you

in line. Besides, you *are* my daughter. At least for the next week until the heat blows off and we can skedaddle to San Francisco.''

"Okay! Let's just find us a hotel room so I can get out of this thing.'' She pulled at the thick cotton dress. "You know how much I hate these grown-up clothes!''

He sighed and picked up the back-breaking bags, wondering again if the 18-year-old girl was worth all this trouble.

Spur stared at the telegram.

SPUR McCOY, QUINTOCH, KANSAS
FRIENDS ARE COMING INTO TOWN
STOP MAN AND WOMAN STOP MAY BE
FATHER AND DAUGHTER STOP HE'S
OLDER, TALL, DARK, GAMBLER STOP
SHE'S SHORT, DARK, PRETTY STOP
RECENTLY PICKED UP 25,000 SHIPMENT
OF GREENS ON THE KANSAS PACIFIC
FROM THE B.E.P. SHIPMENT STOP
DEFINITELY COMING YOUR WAY STOP
URGENT YOU SAY HELLO TO THEM FOR
MOTHER STOP
JIM HALLECK, WASHINGTON, D.C.

He frowned. Though the general had couched the message in cryptic language it wasn't too hard to figure out what his boss was trying to tell him.

"What's that mean?'' Annabelle asked as she read the telegram.

"You being the sheriff's daughter, I guess I can tell you. Seems this man and woman robbed a train. They're coming here and may already be in town. Must have crossed state lines after they did it or I wouldn't have been assigned to it." He rubbed his growling stomach. "They stole twenty-five thousand dollars from a Bureau of Engraving and Printing. The money was probably going to banks in the central U.S. My boss, General Halleck, wants that money back. They may or may not be father and daughter. Looks like I have something else to keep you occupied."

"A woman trainrobber?" Annabelle laughed. "Sounds like something that Kay Fordham would do. She's always saying women can do anything that men can."

"At least one woman's proving her right." Spur shook his head. "After the murder this morning I don't see how I can do both jobs."

She reached between his legs and massaged his over-stuffed crotch. "Oh, I think you're man enough."

He chuckled.

"But, Spur, I know my father's counting on you to find whoever's doing this. Four hangings." She grimaced. "Any more and I don't know what he'll do. Course, I'm not worried because no women have been hanged. But still . . . ."

"I'll just have to do both, won't I? I may not get much sleep for a while but it'll be worth it. Now, did I hear you mention something about food a while back?"

She jumped up and ran to the door.

After the noon meal, Spur started checking the saloons. There were so many men of every description and size gambling, that he couldn't begin to pick out a suspected train robber. Frustrated, he headed for the Quintoch County Bank.

"Yes?"

The man sat at a desk, dip pen poised over the inkwell.

"Hi. I'm helping Sheriff Andrews out with a little problem."

The banker's eyes narrowed. "What kind of a problem?"

"You'd have to ask him about that."

"Hmmmm."

"Has anyone deposited large amounts of cash recently? Say, in the last few days?"

The banker eyed him suspiciously. "I pride myself on being a good judge of character. I think I can trust you. No sir. In fact, just the reverse. Mrs. Tucker drew out her life's savings to buy the old Luria place on Franklin Avenue."

"You're sure?"

"Of course I'm sure!" He doused the pen with ink.

"Thanks for your time."

He started going into store after store. If the thieves had hit Quintoch they'd be spending money like it was water. The first place he hit after the bank was Tomkin's General Hardware. He walked into the dusty shop and blinked to accustom his eyes.

"Yes? Can I help you?"

"Hope so," Spur told the young man. "I'm looking to start a business in town here. I figured since everyone needs hardware I'd come here to ask how folks spend in this town. Is business good?"

Jack Hastings frowned and picked at his front

tooth. "Fact of the matter is, it's been pretty poorly lately. I don't know if Quintoch's the right town for you, sir."

Spur nodded. "So no one's been in lately spending lots of cash?"

Gaines laughed. "Hell, if that'd happen we'd be celebrating!"

"Maybe this isn't the town. Thanks."

Spur walked out into the building sunshine, frustrated. General Halleck definitely wanted the thieves caught before they could spend too much of the money. How was he going to do it?

At least he could check out the saloons again. There was four of them in town. The Bar S was the crudest of the places and would have fit right in a wild frontier town. It was a small, one-room saloon. Its bar consisted of a plank set up on two old barrels. A row of pegs behind it held the drinkers' weapons.

"Why do you make the men give up their hoglegs?" Spur asked the barkeep.

"Ain't no trouble in the Bar S," the greasy man said. "I aim to keep it that way. If you're here to drink hand it over!" He extended a fat paw over the plank.

"No, just looking for a friend."

The dirt floor was covered with wood shavings, broken here and there by a few nicked chairs that held snoring cowboys. The Bar S was strictly for serious drinking men and didn't seem a likely place for the thief to go.

Spur checked two more places, watching the men who sat hunched over their cards, faces taut, emotionless as they played. None of them were particularly well dressed; none were flashing around large sums of money and none were old enough to fit General Halleck's cryptic description.

He finally went to the Prairie King. It was the nicest of the gambling establishments. It had a dance floor, plenty of tables, pretty women, lots of liquor and a passable piano-player, an amiable guy whom everyone called Keno. Probably from his favorite game, Spur thought, as he sidled up to the bar. Though he wasn't there to drink, he had to fit in, so he nursed his whiskey and looked around.

Two fancy ladies, bored and hot, cooled themselves with ostrich feather fans.

Fancy ladies, Spur thought. Perhaps the thief had visited one of them. What was the name of the one who'd told him her sad story?

The two women saw Spur looking at them and misinterpreted his interest. They jumped to their feet and sashayed over to him. A sad-faced, bodice-busting woman grabbed their dresses and yanked them back. They squealed.

"Ain't nothin' doing," she said. "Just go back there and rest yer backs for a spell. This one's mine, girls!"

"Oh Gussie, we seen him first!" a pretty woman in a peach and white dress said.

"Yeah. You just wanna steal him from us! You don't need him!"

"Like hell! He's my steady. I've already had him two times." Her eyes flashed. "Now git!" Gussie strode over to him at the bar.

"Hello again," he said.

She was panting. "Howdy. A girl's sure gotta watch out for her own interests here. They was ready to eat you alive! Course, I wanted to have the chance to do that myself!''

Spur looked at her, all flushed, eyes sparkling, expectant. ''Do you have a room?'' he asked, and set down his drink.

Gussie laughed. ''Do I have a room?'' She grabbed his arm and pulled him to the stairs, tossing her head at her two competitors as she passed them.

Moments later they were inside. She turned up the kerosene lamp, since the window was covered with red damask drapes. ''I sure am glad you changed your mind,'' Gussie said. ''Should I take 'em off or you wanna do that?''

Spur sat on the bed. ''Leave them on.''

The whore squealed. ''Oooh, you sure are a crazy one! You want me to pull up my dress?''

''No. Sit beside me, Gussie.'' Spur patted the quilt next to him.

She sighed and settled down on it. ''So?''

''How's business been lately, Gussie?''

The woman rolled her eyes. ''Oh lordy; you're not one of them talkers, is you? Why don't you just do what you came up here to do.''

''I am. Fact is, I'm a businessman. I'm thinking of opening up a saloon right here in Quintoch.''

''I—I see.''

Spur spun his story as he told it. ''Yes ma'am. That's why I'm here, seeing if this town could use another saloon.''

She held up her hands as if to ward off a blow. ''Don't go talking to me about it.'' She stood and walked to the cracked mirror that hung beside the wall lamp. ''Soon as I can I'm getting out of his hell-hole. I got sweet talked into doing this once but it won't happen again." She poked at her reddish-brown hair.

"You misunderstand me, Gussie. I wanna know how much this place earns. How much you earn."

She turned to him and straightened her back. "One to two dollars a customer—depending on how he's dressed."

"I see. Ever make more than that?"

"Sure! Lots of times!" Gussie looked at the carpet. "Well, once in a while. Feller was in here not more than an hour ago. He gave me a twenty dollar bill for a quick one. Billy—he's the pipsqueak who hired me—lets us set our own prices. I saw this man, sized him up, figured he had money. I asked for five dollars. And he gave me twenty!"

"Not bad." There weren't many men willing to spend that kind of money for a woman, no matter how long it had been since they saw one. It was a possibility. "What'd this man look like?"

Gussie frowned. "Why you wanna know?"

"Sounds like a possible competitor. Maybe he's thinking the same thing I am. He might've been trying you out." Or maybe he was spending new money he'd just pulled off the Kansas Pacific Railroad.

"Oh, hell, I don't know. He was tall, skinny, maybe around fifty." She sighed. "Reminded me of my daddy."

"That's all you remember?"

She scrunched her eyebrows. "Clean shaven. None of those whiskers to chew up my face. And no moustache." She sat beside him again. "I also remember that you wanted to come up to my room. Whether we did nothing or not I gotta get paid." Gussie held out her hand. "If I don't come to him with money that pipsqueak boss of mine says he'll hit me."

Spur gave her a ten dollar bill.

"Land sakes!" the whore said. "You sure are a nice man!" She smooched his left cheek.

"You have many men like this rich one?"

"No. Lots of them are real strange. Like last night. This guy, who I recalled seein' around town once in t'while, took me up here. He didn't do nothing—didn't even talk. He just had me drop my dress and bloomers and looked at me. Finally he said something about 'momma,' gave me a dollar and ran out!" She blew out her breath. "Business really has been different!" Gussie stroked his thigh. "You sure you don't want nothing for your ten dollars?"

He smiled. "That's okay. I think I've gotten enough. Thanks, Miss Granger."

She rolled her eyes. "It's been a long time since anyone called me miss!"

Spur left her room and walked to the sheriff's office. Maybe Andrews could help him. Maybe the sheriff had some ideas about these train robbers.

Andrews was gruff. "Hell, I don't know nothing about that," he said. "So many people here in this town it'd be like tryin' to find a virgin over the age of fifteen!"

McCoy laughed and slid into the chair.

"So what're you doing about the hangings?" the sheriff asked.

"Not much right now. Investigating. Asking questions. I'm all tied up with these train thieves."

"You say you got a telegram? From Washington?"

"Yep."

Jonathan Andrews groaned. "And so now you can't look for the man who's been murdering my citizens. Is that the way it is?"

"Only for a while." Sheriff sure was acting strange, Spur thought. "No more than a few days."

"We could have ten more hangings in that time."

"My superiors decided that this takes priority."

"Well, I don't like that." Andrews rose to his feet. "I don't like that one bit. If I didn't know better I'd say there was something fishy going on here."

"Sheriff?" Spur said as the man walked behind him.

"Sure seems nice and tidy." He whistled.

Spur heard someone approaching from the jail behind him. He didn't bother turning around until his arms were pulled behind him. Steel jaws clamped around his wrists before he could begin to react.

"Hey!" he yelled.

"Spur McCoy, you're under arrest!"

CHAPTER EIGHT

Spur stood, struggling against the biting handcuffs. "What the hell do you think you're doing, Andrews? Have you gone out of your head?"

"I'm doing what I shoulda done first time I met you," Sheriff Andrews said. He glanced at his deputy, who stood smiling, arms crossed over his chest, staring at his handiwork. "Good job, Watson."

"Sheriff Andrews, you're not thinking straight." Spur let his bound hands fall to his back. "You've been blaming yourself for all the neck-tie parties going on in your town. You're not to blame and neither am I!"

He laughed. "Sure, McCoy." The sheriff's eyes were wild. "Why didn't I see it before? You must've come into town earlier and started killing the men. Then, for some reason you got scared so you came to me with that idiotic story about working for Washington. What bullshit! I believed you then—but not now." The sheriff rubbed his bald spot and turned to his deputy. "Watson, throw this killer in the left cell!"

"Yessir!"

"Yeah," Spur said to the young man as he hustled him into the jail. "And then go to room five at the Diamond Ridge Hotel. Look under my mattress. You'll find the telegram I just got today about the train thieves!"

"Good try, McCoy! You talk big, I'll give you that. Almost fooled me too."

Spur turned to the deputy. "Just do it!"

Watson shoved Spur into the cell and slammed it shut. His nimble fingers turned the key and yanked it out.

"Well, sheriff, what's the harm in it?" Watson asked.

"What's the harm in what?" he exploded.

"Might as well search his room. We would anyway—to see if there's anything in there worth taking—I mean, that might prove he's the killer."

"Oh hell! Alright." Andrews walked up to Spur, who pressed himself against the bars. "But I know we won't find anything that'll get you outa there. You ain't going nowhere, Spur McCoy!"

Spur banged his shoulders against the steel shafts.

The room opened and closed. "Did you do it? Did you go and do it like you said you were?"

Vincent Vandemere winced. "Hell, girl; keep your voice down! You want the whole hotel to know? These walls are as thin as your maidenhood!"

"I don't got my maidenhood anymore!" Maddie said in a shrill voice. "You took it from me!" She slammed the door.

"That's what I mean! Now pipe down!"

Maddie sighed and sat on the bed. "Well? Did you go and do it or not?"

"Yes. Rode out two hours ago. Hid it where no one'll ever find it."

"Not all of it!" Maddie said, eyes wide. "Vince, you didn't go and do something stupid like that! I gotta have some money to enjoy this town!"

"Of course not! I kept out a hundred apiece—just like we agreed." How could an 18-year-old girl be so loud, he wondered as he pulled the stack of crisp ten dollar bills from the pillow.

"Goody! Then I can buy some new dresses." She gazed at the money and frowned. "Doesn't seem like much when you think about what we have. Why couldn't you have kept out four hundred?"

"You know why. We can't go and spend up the town. Someone would notice us." He leaned closer to her. "They will be looking for us."

Maddie punched his gut. "No one would ever notice you Vince, darling. You're old and ugly."

"Well, they'd notice you. And stop calling me that! Might as well get in practice."

"Okay, daddy dear!" Maddie grabbed the money and squealed. "We're gonna leave tomorrow, right?"

"No! Three days from now we catch the westbound train for Denver. Then we go all the way west."

She sighed. "If we make it." Maddie let the bills drop from her fingers.

"We will make it! If you can keep your mouth shut, child!" He looked at her harshly. "One slip of yer tongue and it's all over for us."

"I know, I know." Maddie played with the money, running a polished fingernail up and down the rectangles. "I just git all excited."

Vincent frowned. "Just stop getting excited around me."

Maddie whooped. "Why, daddy dear, I thought I'd never hear you say that!"

He sighed. "You know what I mean!"

"Yeah. I know." The girl glanced at the curtain-draped window. "Are we really safe here?"

Vincent Vandermere shrugged. "As safe as any place. Look, go out and buy yourself a new dress. I have some thinking to do."

"Okay." She kissed his forehead. "Goodbye, father."

Spur sat in the cell, cursing Annabelle's father. He knew the pressures the man had been suffering through, but that didn't make his current situation any easier to take. He had too much to do—find the thieves, stop the hangings—to spend the afternoon locked up.

McCoy watched a well-fed prairie mouse poke out from a hole in the wall, sniff the air and skitter across the floor until it had cleared the bars. If only he could get out that easily.

The front door banged shut.

"Well, what is it, Watson?" he heard Sheriff Andrews say. "I don't got all day!"

"You better look at this." The deputy's voice was

dark. "Found it right where he said I would—under his bed in the hotel."

Paper rustled. Silence. The sheriff exploded. "Damn!"

"Yessir."

"Well, I can't make heads nor tails outa this, but it sure ain't a normal telegram. Unless he's got a deal with Mr. Drake—which I can't believe—I guess he might be who he says he is. What's all this mean?"

Spur walked up to the bars. "You can't read it because it's in code," he yelled and waited. Soon enough the sheriff appeared.

"Talk!"

McCoy sighed. "My boss doesn't send telegrams describing train thieves. Any telegraph operator along the line could have picked up his message. Some of them are crooked and we don't want this information being spread around. So, while it's plain to me what it means, it wouldn't be to most other men."

Sheriff Andrews frowned and studied it. "I could see how it might be. Don't make any sense to me."

"Shouldn't we—ah—" Watson began.

"Hell, you trying to do my job?"

"No, sir. No sir!"

Andrews hesitated. "Well, hell. I guess I just lost myself a killer." He threw the keys to Watson.

"You never had one." Spur stepped back as the deputy unlocked the door. "Now the cuffs, if you don't mind."

"All right!"

A bit of maneuvering and two clicks later, Spur was rubbing his wrists. "No real harm done, sheriff."

Andrews reached for the bottle on his desk. "Hell, sorry, McCoy. I guess I went crazy there. It's this town. Kay Fordham's been by here three times today, worried she'll find another body. She's up in arms and it wouldn't surprise me a bit if she starts roaming the streets at night with that Spencer of hers."

Spur opened his mouth. "Kay has a rifle?"

Andrews nodded. "Damn right!" He slumped in his chair, the whiskey forgotten in one hand. "Hell, Spur; I'm afraid if I don't track down the killer soon the good people of this town'll turn nasty. They'll take the law into their own hands. We may yet have another lynching—" He frowned.

"What about this Mike Hughes? Know anything about him?"

The sheriff nodded. "His mother died bringing him into the world. Father got killed by a Southerner during the war. Mike inherited their ranch, but he sold it when he came back. Been living on the proceeds ever since, not doing much of anything besides drinking and cards."

"Have you considered that the killer might well be one of their own?"

Andrews stared at Spur and laughed. "Yeah. Hell; I've even wondered if I've been doing it. But I don't see the reasoning. And Mike Hughes looked scared to death that night he came to see me."

"Maybe he was scared he'd kill another one of his friends. Maybe he can't control himself."

"Maybe."

"Well, sheriff, I gotta find me some train thieves. You keep in touch. And get some rest!"

"I got my rest right here." He poured a glass of the amber colored liquid and drank it down.

Spur walked out into the sunshine. Time enough for the hangings later. Halleck gave the train thieves priority. He passed a shop filled with women's finery. He glanced in the window and grunted. It was worth a try.

The middleaged storeowner shook her head. "No, sir. We haven't had no fancy women in lately—except Gussie. She keeps on coming in to have her dresses mended." The double-chinned woman propped her glasses higher on her nose as she laughed. "I can't imagine how that poor dear keeps on tearing 'em! Course I don't mind the business. Her boss pays for it."

"Well, it wouldn't have to be a fancy lady. Just some young woman with lots of money."

"No. Don't rightly remember. Sorry, mister."

He tipped his hat. "Thank you." Spur hurried to the next store that catered to women—a milliner. It made sense. A young woman with plenty of cash would naturally get some new things, as long as she wasn't a woman like the rifle-toting Kay Fordham.

Sarah's Fine Hat Shop was closed. A sign on the door read: "Back in one hour. Picking up New Shipment imported Ostrich Feathers from train."

Spur pushed on and finally found a second dress shop: Tillie's Tailor Made Creations for Ladies. The dresses in the multi-paned window showed that Tillie was a better than average seamstress.

He went into the small store. A woman was dusting a mannekin. Spur walked directly to her.

"Sorry to bother you, ma'am."

Kay Fordham turned around. "Spur McCoy! I'll bet you're wondering what a woman like me's doing in a store like this."

He nodded. "Matter of fact, I was. Doesn't seem to be your kind of place. You don't wear this stuff."

Kay grimaced. "Tillie's a new friend. I'm trying to get her to join my society. Anyway, she had to go off and help birth a baby—she's the local midwife—and she asked me to watch her store for her. Normally she would've closed, but the train just came in and she wanted to catch the business." Kay looked squarely at him. "So what brings you in here? Something about them hangings?"

"Ah—well—something like that."

Kay laughed throatily. "Heck, old Jonathan told me everything. Don't worry, my lips are sealed."

"Just how much did he tell you about me?"

"Enough."

"Actually, I'm wondering if a young woman came in here today. Very young. With a lot of money."

The woman eyed him suspiciously. "Land sakes, man! Ain't me and Annabelle enough for you?"

He laughed. Was there anything the woman didn't know?

"She'd be spending brand new money. Not some old bills that've spent the last year folded up in some cowboy's pocket."

Kay touched the feather duster to his nose. "Aren't you gonna tell me why you're looking for this here woman?"

"Why should I bother?" He sneezed. "You'll just

find out anyway." McCoy brushed it aside. "Has a woman like that come in here? Come on, Kay. It's important!"

"Yes. I may have seen the woman you're talking about. She stormed in here, all wrapped up in the gaudiest.... Well, I showed her two dresses and she picked both of them. They're in the back waiting for Tillie to alter them to her size. She must've been about eighteen, I'd say. But an *old* eighteen. If I could just get her to dress plainly she might be the kind of woman who'd understand what I talk about," the suffragette said. "Anyway, she never asked the price of anything. Said she'll pay in cash."

"Did she leave her name? Where's she staying?"

"Let's see." Kay went to the table in the back of the shop and checked the ledger. "Yep! Here it is." She closed the leather-bound book and slammed her hand down on it. "What do I get if I tell you?"

"Come on, Kay; I don't have the time for that!"

"Mr. McCoy—" she began.

"Using feminine wiles on me, are you?" Spur moved close to her. "I didn't think you did things like that to men." His voice was flat.

Kay's cheeks colored. "Alright. You caught me. But you can't blame a woman for trying!" She looked at the ledger, studying it with her sea-green eyes. "Jennie Clowshare."

"Does it say where she's staying?"

"No, of course not. She's supposed to pick up the dresses tomorrow morning." Kay fixed her eyes on Spur. "Just what is this all about?"

"Sorry, Kay. I got business to do." He pecked her cheek and walked toward to the door, dodging yards of lace and feather-strewn hats.

"Spur McCoy!" she yelled, exasperated. "What am I gonna do with you?"

"Whatever you want—as long as it doesn't involve that rifle of yours." He stopped and looked back at her.

The woman gaped. "Who told you—"

"You're not the only one the sheriff tells everything to." He grinned and walked out.

Jenny Clowshare probably wasn't her real name, if she was the girl he was hunting for. He stood on the street, hands on his hips. There were three decent hotels in town, one rooming house and a few he wouldn't wish on his enemies. Spur bolted toward the closest one—the Livingston.

The front desk man was out, so Spur flipped through the registry. He searched the barely legible scrawls. No Clowshares.

He got lucky at the next establishment. Mr. Frederick Clowshare and Miss Jennifer Clowshare were registered in room 311. He glanced at the stairs and, seeing a dark-suited man coming toward the desk, McCoy casually walked to the landing.

He checked the tilt of his hat in the shiny spittoon that sat on the newelpost and made his way up the stairs. He nodded to an elegantly dressed couple on their way down, but the white haired woman didn't fit General Halleck's description of the train robbers.

He made the third floor and checked the closest room, 306, just in the middle of the corridor. Spur found the room he wanted and tapped lightly on the door. No answer. He knocked again, harder. Still nothing from inside.

The hall was empty so Spur checked the knob. It was locked. He removed his billfold, pulled back the lining and extracted a small set of skeleton keys. The first one did the trick. The latch clicked and the knob turned in his hand.

He went in quickly, stashing the keys and his wallet in his back pocket under his coat tails. The room was filled with carpet bags. The velvet and oak chairs were draped with women's undergarments and the closets were stuffed with dresses.

Spur sighed and searched the room, working quickly but neatly so that its occupants wouldn't know someone had been through their belongings.

After five minutes he hadn't come up with much. He'd found 100 dollars in new, crisp bills—that was all. They'd been printed in Washington D.C. and were uncirculated. Jenny and Frederick Clowshare—whatever their real names were—must be his thieves.

He pocketed the money and returned the room to its normal appearance. McCoy stepped out, closed the door and locked it with the skeleton key.

He slipped down the stairs and went outside. Somewhere in this booming town were two people who'd robbed the U.S. Government of $25,000.

Hundreds of men and women walked the streets and breezed by in buckboards and buggies. Young mothers comforted screaming babies. Merchants were shining their windows with fleeces. Couples walked arm in arm.

At least he knew where to start looking, McCoy thought, gazing at the confusion. He leaned against the hitching post that fronted the Livingston Hotel.

He'd be at Tillie's shop in the morning, waiting for a young woman to pick up her new dresses.

Hands slipped around his throat, squeezing, choking.

CHAPTER NINE

"I oughta kill you!"

His attacker's voice was soft and feminine. Spur pried the strangling hands from his neck and swung their owner in front of him.

"I should kill you, you know," Annabelle Andrews said. "Running off like that!"

Spur laughed and rubbed his throat. "Sorry, Annabelle."

"Where you been?"

"I had a little run-in with your father."

She rolled her eyes. "My father?"

He stood. "Yep. He had me under arrest for a while this afternoon. And I've been busy—"

Annabelle whooped. "Serves you right! You deserve to be locked up for what you did to me!"

"Annabelle!"

A portly man dressed in overalls and dirt walked up to their little scene. "Can I help you, ma'am?" He spat brown juice and warily eyed Spur. "This man bothering you?"

She hesitated and smiled. "Not really, but thanks."

The high-nosed man squinted at her. "You just say the word and I'll flatten him!" He raised a fist.

"No, really, it's nothing!" She grabbed Spur's arm. "See? We're just having a disagreement."

"Okay. It's your funeral." He shook his head and walked away.

"I guess that's just what I needed to liven up a boring day."

The sheriff's daughter frowned. "I'm sorry, Spur, but as soon as you left I got so hot I couldn't stand it." She shook her head. "Took three cold baths but that didn't help a whit! So when I saw you sitting there, doing nothing, torturing me, I just thought I'd get your attention."

"You got it alright. Annabelle, I have work to do. You know that." He touched her right cheek. "I'll get back to you as soon as I can."

"Work? You're just sitting around!"

"Annabelle, I've—I've—" His words trailed off. A man and a young woman were approaching the Livingston Hotel.

Maddie yanked on Frederick Vandermeer's arm. "Come on!" the girl yelled. "I just have to have something to eat! I'm starving!"

"Can't you ever just talk? The way you scream you'd think I was half a mile away." Vandermeer stopped walking and stared at her. "Maddie—I mean Jennie—you're driving me up the wall!"

"You're so tall it's a short trip." She stuck out her tongue at him.

He sighed. "Sometimes I wonder if this was the

right idea. Getting you involved in all this.''

Maddie smiled. ''Really? You didn't seem to mind two days ago when I distracted the guards on the train! Didn't I come in handy, daddy dear, by accidentally losing my dress in front of those four men and falling to the floor in a dead faint?'' She laughed.

''I'll admit, you played your part.'' He dabbed sweat from his chin. ''But it's high time you changed your tune. Remember, you're my daughter, a sweet, virginal girl from back east. Try to act like that!''

''How can I? You've ruined me for life!'' She dramatically slapped the back of her hand to her bonnet. ''Led me into a world of guns and money and sex! I'm a changed woman, Frederick; changed beyond belief. And I'll never forgive you.''

''Maddie!'' He said the word through gritted teeth.

''Until just before we split the money. Then I'll forgive you.''

''Let's just get back to the hotel. I'm out of cash—for some reason.'' He eyed the sparkling amethyst pendant that hung around the girl's neck. ''Then we'll get some dinner.''

''You've what?'' Annabelle demanded.

''Like I said, I've got work to do.''

They sure looked like the right people, Spur thought, eyeing the tall man and young woman as they argued on the other side of the street. Her dress was expensive; his suit tailor-made. She still had the dewy cheeks of youth.

''Spur McCoy, you're impossible!''

"Impossible?" he asked, still looking at the pair.

They'd stopped fighting and were crossing the broad avenue, avoiding the steaming horse droppings that littered the dusty road.

"Impossible to make!" Annabelle blurted.

"I'll see you later, missy!"

"All right! I'll never cook for you if you keep this up!"

The well dressed couple passed by him and disappeared inside the Livingston Hotel lobby. Spur nodded to Annabelle, waited two seconds and walked in.

They were headed up the stairs. He followed at a discrete distance, taking his time, rounding each landing just as they moved up the next flight.

He watched them walk onto the third floor. So far so good. At the top of the stairs Spur glanced to the right down the hall. The door to room 311 closed.

That was them. He didn't need to wait until the morning to settle this. He could do it right now.

Spur dashed down the hall and pounded on the door.

"What the hell is it?" a gruff voice said. "My daughter and I are exhausted!"

"Fire!"

"What?"

Spur pushed his mouth to the thin door. "There's a fire in the hotel! Get out now to save your lives!"

"A fire? Vincent, no!"

It was the girl's voice. He heard some rustling from the room. The door finally opened.

"What's this about a fire?" the tall, dignified man said. "I don't smell smoke."

"It hasn't started yet." Spur pushed past him, entered the room and slammed the door behind him.

"What's the meaning of this?"

"Vincent—I mean daddy—!"

The 18-year-old girl grabbed the dress from the floor. She held it up to cover her bloomers and bodice.

"Settle down, folks," Spur said. "There's no fire, but there will be one if you don't cooperate."

"Cooperate? You can't barge in here and threaten us!"

"Sit down!" Spur drew his Colt .45. "Both of you! On the bed!"

"Vincent?"

"Damn!"

Spur followed the man's eyes to the holster draped around the doorknob behind him. "Not a smart move, mister."

"Tell me something I don't know."

"Shut up!" He spat the words. "Where'd you hide it?"

The man and woman looked at each other.

"Hide what?" she asked.

"You wanna play games?" He cocked the revolver. "I got all day."

"We don't know what you're talking about." The man straightened up on the bed. "My daughter and I are traveling to San Francisco. Her aunt died and we're to attend her funeral."

"Good story. Now where'd you hide the money? It's not in your room, I checked it."

The girl opened her mouth.

"Come on."

"Are you trying to rob us?"

Spur laughed. "I'm an agent of the Secret Service. They put me on your trail. Seems they're missing twenty-five thousand dollars. A couple who look an awful lot like you took it from the Kansas Pacific train a few days ago."

"You dare insult us with your accusations?" He rose.

"Git your butt down!" Spur waved the weapon in the air. "You can sit there until you drop dead, but I'd rather get this over with. Where is it?"

The girl was pale. She watched the man nervously, fidgeting with the scarlet dress that she'd lain in her lap. Maybe he could work on her.

"Sir, we can sit here until doomsday. We don't know what you're talking about."

"That's—that's right." The young woman's voice was hesitant.

"I went through your room a few minutes ago. Found five brand new twenty-dollar bills. Uncirculated. Fresh from the Bureau of Engraving and Printing. How do you suppose they got in your carpetbag?"

"You're lying!"

"Vincent," the girl began.

"Shut your mouth, Maddie!"

"No, Vincent, I can't stand it anymore." The girl stood. "I have to get out of these clothes!"

Spur watched the man as the girl lifted the bodice from her body. "Maddie? Maddie and Vincent?" he said, deliberately ignoring the girl. "I thought your names were Jennifer and Frederick."

The man sat tensely on the bed. Spur glanced at Maddie. She was lowering her bloomers, revealing her luscious, young body.

"Sorry, honey, that won't work." Spur kicked the dress to the woman. "Put it on. Now!"

"No!"

"Maddie!"

Spur lowered his aim on the man. "If you don't tell me where you hid the money I'll shoot your knees off. You'll be a cripple for the rest of your life, Vincent!"

He flinched and turned to the girl. "Maddie, get dressed." He sighed. "I guess it's over."

The naked girl gasped. "No, it isn't!" She threw herself at Spur.

He easily sidestepped, maintaining his aim. The girl flopped against the far wall and gasped at the impact.

"Talk!" he yelled.

Vincent sighed. "It's—it's not here."

"Obviously! Where is it?"

Dazed, Maddie made her way to the bed and dropped down on it, all curves and mounds and soft, pink flesh.

The man's face was stony. "Three miles out of town. I hid it near a clump of cottonwoods beside an old ranch." He sighed. "Take the east trail out of town and turn left at the first windmill."

Spur weakly smiled. "I thought you looked like a sensible man."

Maddie raised her head and grinned hopefully at Spur.

He turned back to the man. "Get your whore dressed, Vincent. I don't buy your story. We're all gonna go on a little ride—together!"

The girl's smile faded.

CHAPTER TEN

"Were you a good boy today?"

"Yes, mama."

"You know ah won't bake you no pecan pies if you weren't a good little boy!"

"I was mama. I was!"

Gussie Grainer sighed and pulled at her dress. Her room above the saloon seemed hotter than ever. Why couldn't he just do it to her like all the other men? Acting like this crazy guy's mother was tiring her out.

She'd been at it for 15 minutes while he crawled around on the floor in his longjohns, babbling away about his mother and the plantation. He'd even asked her to "talk Southern-like," so she drawled with the best of them.

She suddenly remembered her own mother. When Gussie had told her she wanted to become an actress the white-haired woman had threatened to jump off the roof. Now here she was, acting her heart out, making three dollars the hard way.

"Mama? Are you still there?" Jack Hastings asked, his voice cracking.

No, I'm not, Gussie thought. But money was money. Every dollar got her closer to home. "Yes, honey. Ah'm right heah." She struggled for something to say. "Don't the—the marigolds smell sweet-ah today!"

He looked up at her from the floor. "Magnolias!" he thundered. "They were goddamn magnolias!"

"Alright, alright, sugar. You can't expect me to remember everything!"

Jack twisted up his face in seeming confusion. "Yes, mama." He bent down and licked the pearl buttons on her boots.

Oh lordy, do I need a drink, Gussie thought. "Look, deah, do you want your mama to take off her dress right now? It sure is hot in heah."

"Okay!" He looked up at her like a puppy.

Gussie closed her eyes. Please, let him stick it in and get the hell out. She took off her clothes as her customer stared up at her from the floor. His face didn't change as she stepped out of the dress, shrugged off the lace chemise and her bloomers. He just kept his sad eyes locked on her, unseeing, almost as if he was blind.

"Ah do declar-ah," Gussie said. "That's much bettah." She stretched, showing off her breasts to their best advantage. That usually did it.

"Mama?" Jack Hastings shot his head from side to side as if he was looking for her.

"Honey, I'm right here! I mean heah!"

"Mama, where are you? Where are you?"

Jeez, this guy's weird. "Look, Jack, what in Hades is going on?"

"Mama?"

"Shut up!"

"The squirrel, mama! The squirrel!"

"Now look, mister, I don't mind doing some strange things, like taking it up the ass, but this is too bizarre for me! Either shove it up me or pay and get out!" Gussie folded her arms on her naked chest.

"But the plantation!" he said desperately. Jack Hastings grabbed her boots. "Please, mama! I'm not ready to leave you yet!"

"No!" She kicked him away and picked up his pants. Three dollar bills were folded together in the front right pocket of the man's worn Levi's. Gussie tucked the money under her pillow and sat on it. "You just used up all your time, honey. See you later."

"Come on, mama!" Jack rose to his knees. He held out his hands to her.

Gussie shook her head. "No way! I can't do it! No more mama, no more pecan pie, no more plantation and no more marigolds!"

Jack Hastings winced. "Magnolias!"

"Whatever!"

"Go ahead and put on your dress, Maddie," Vincent Vandermeer said.

She sighed. "I knew this would happen!" She started for the closet.

"No, the red one!" He pointed to the dress she'd worn earlier that day, mounds of stiff taffeta.

She looked at him.

"No sense in dirtying up another one of those expensive do-dads!"

"Okay. What about my others?" She pointed to

her underthings.

"No time for that," Spur said. "Just hurry!"

He leaned against the door, feeling the man's holster pressing against his hips. "Pretty good idea, using her," he said to Vincent, who sat on the bed, hands folded on his knees. "Your biggest mistake was coming into this town."

"I know that now. Have to rub it in?"

Maddie had made herself as decent as she could. She turned around, showing Spur a slice of bare skin between the unbuttoned flaps. "Would you help a girl out?" she asked sweetly.

"No. Why don't you have your *father* help you?"

"Oh, alright. Come on, Vincent."

The man rose and walked to her.

"Turn sideways and don't try anything, girl!" Spur said.

The man dutifully fastened the buttons into their cloth slots. Spur didn't believe the man had given up. He'd try something, sometime. And so would the girl.

"How old is she anyway, Vincent?"

"Eighteen."

"Uh-huh. And how old was she the first time you—"

"Eighteen!" The 50-year-old man fumbled with the buttons. "I've only known this paragon of virtue for six months. Six months of heaven and hell!" He finished the last one.

"Let's go."

Spur made Vincent lead the way, keeping the girl on a short leash. "You try anything and I'll shoot you," he whispered.

The girl nodded and walked down the stairs.

They didn't give him any trouble as they went to Henry's Livery stable. There Spur rented a serviceable buckboard and two rested horses to pull it. When it came time to talk money, Vincent Vandermeer—Spur had finally learned his last name—pulled a new 20-dollar bill from his pocket. McCoy quickly snatched it from the man's hands and paid Henry with good circulated currency.

Soon they were bouncing out of town. The sun was two hours down from noon in the sky. He made Vincent handle the reins with Maddie sitting beside him. Spur rode in the back seat, keeping his Colt trained on the man's back.

Two cowboys on horseback approached them on the trail. "Keep your mouth shut, sweetheart," he said to Maddie. She dutifully did so as they waved and passed on by.

They ate dust for a while, moving through the brown cloud that the horses had kicked up. It must not have rained in Quintoch for quite a while, judging from the haze that filled the air.

Maddie started sneezing. "Achoo. Achoo. Excuse me."

"Stop that, Maddie."

She did. "Vincent, there must be some way we can get out of this."

"Hey, lawman, what're your plans for us after we give you the money?"

"Have the county sheriff lock you up. I'm sure you'll get a fair trial." Spur ignored the rumbling in his stomach. He sure could have used the lunch Annabelle promised him hours ago.

"Trial? All we did was take a few lousy bucks!"

Maddie said.

"Twenty-five thousand, to be exact."

"So? What's the big deal?" Maddie asked. "We're giving it back."

Spur glanced at the back of her head. "That's right. It'll look good. Maybe the judge'll take that into account, as well as your, uh, tender years, Maddie."

"But what about Vincent?"

"I couldn't say."

"Will you two shut your mouths?" Vincent said. "Just drive."

They rode in silence. A half hour later Spur saw a ranch to the south. A windmill, half its vanes torn off, flapped from side to side in the light breeze. The buckboard continued on down the trail.

Vincent looked over his shoulder at Spur and shrugged. "So I lied."

"I figured."

Ten minutes later eight horseshoes bit into the sandy soil. Vincent drove them out onto the prairie, past clumps of yellow and white flowers. Spur saw the clean tracks that showed someone else had recently been here.

"You better be taking me to the money," Spur warned him.

"I am. Believe me! And it'll be a relief to get Maddie off my hands! Even jail's better than her!"

"That's so rude! Vincent, you oaf!" She slapped him.

"Cut it out!"

The horseshoe prints tracked back near a clump of straggly trees. Vincent reined in the beasts and sighed. "This is it. This is where I hid the money."

Keeping his Colt trained on the man's back, Spur surveyed the ground. Darker soil was spilled onto the lighter top layer of dirt. Someone had moved it. Maybe Vincent was telling him the truth.

McCoy jumped out and stood beside the buckboard. "Okay. Out. Both of you!" he barked.

Vincent tried to hand the reins to him. Spur waved him off with his weapon so the man dropped them and stepped onto the ground. Maddie huffed her way out at the same time.

"Dig, Vincent! Use your hands, since we didn't bring a shovel!"

The man laughed. "Don't need one. It's right there in those trees, between their trunks. I found a mighty fine place to hide it. You'd never think there was anything in there if you didn't know."

Spur looked. The slender trunks formed a dense jungle. Inside, it was dark and there seemed to be plenty of room. But he didn't like it.

"Okay. Take it out and let's get going."

Vincent hesitated. "I'd rather not do that."

"Why not?"

The man looked at Maddie and shrugged.

"Then we'll have her do it!" He motioned her over to the clump of cottonwoods with his revolver. "Go on, Maddie, get the money."

"No, Maddie! I—ah—" He bent down and handed her a dead tree trunk. "Shove this in there first!"

"Why, Vincent?"

"Girl, just do it!"

Spur watched her. Maddie clutched the thick

branch. "Lord, this thing's heavy!" She swallowed hard and poked it into the dark opening. "You put a snake in there or something?"

"Or something."

Two metallic clanks sounded from the trees. Maddie yelled and dropped the stick.

Vincent sighed. "It's okay. Pull it out now."

The girl tugged on the branch, revealing two bear-traps. Their shiny jaws had nearly bitten through the four-inch-thick wood.

"Nice, Vincent. Not very original, but effective." Spur said. "Get the bags!"

Maddie bent down.

"Not you, him! Come on, Vandermeer!"

The girl stepped back. Vincent knelt beside the trunks, pushed away the deadly traps and reached into the pocket formed by the trees.

"Well?" Spur asked.

"I'm looking." He scrunched up his face, moving his arm back and forth.

"I'm warning you, Vincent!"

"Ah. There they are!" He hauled out one bag and sat it on the dirt.

Spur relaxed as the next three emerged from their hiding place. The large canvas bags were stuffed so full the man had barely gotten them tied shut. Vincent looked up at him. "Well? What now?"

McCoy blew out his breath. It was almost over. "Put them in the buckboard. You and Maddie have an appointment with Sheriff Andrews." Spur glanced toward her. The 18-year-old girl was fumbling with her skirt.

"What's wrong, Maddie?" Spur asked.

She smiled up at him. "Nothing's wrong—with me."

"Maddie!" her partner called.

"Vincent! Use your gun!"

Spur turned toward the man. In that instant an explosion rocked the air. Hot lead tore into his left shoulder. The searing metal burned a hole in his flesh, ripped through veins and grazed muscles before it blasted out the other side.

Stunned, Spur looked at the girl. She smiled and showed him her derringer as Vincent tackled him, grabbing for his Colt .45.

CHAPTER ELEVEN

Vincent Vandermeer knocked the Colt from Spur's hand. The Secret Service agent ignored the fire burning in his torn shoulder and elbowed Vincent's midsection. The man backed up, doubled over in pain. Spur scrambled for the gun.

"Hurry up and kill him!" Maddie said.

Vandermeer launched his body from the sand and slammed down on top of Spur's revolver. McCoy lunged for him. Vincent rolled onto his back and threw the Colt to Maddie.

His shoulder wouldn't work properly. The burn turned to a cold numbness as shock set into his bullet-pierced flesh. Spur shook his head and turned toward the girl. Maddie aimed at his heart, gripping the Colt .45 with both hands.

"Kill him!" Vincent said.

She laughed. "No, he's too cute. Just beat him up and let's get the hell outa here!"

"Damn you!"

The man slugged Spur's wounded left shoulder. It exploded in pain. He groaned in renewed agony

and twisted around to face his attacker. Spur got
off one solid punch to the jaw but Vincent easily
recovered and slammed his fist into McCoy's
oozing wound.

Pain blinded him. He couldn't block it out. It
slammed into his brain, disorienting him. McCoy
stumbled around, struggling to regain his senses.

"Do it!" Vincent yelled.

Something hard crashed down on his skull. Spur
groaned and dropped to his knees, groggy, aching,
every nerve in his body screaming.

"Again!"

Another solid whack. He slumped to the hot dirt.
His vision blurred.

Then he saw nothing at all.

Sand coated his lips. The sun burned down on
him. Spur coughed, wiped his lips and sat up. He
felt the big lump on his head and realized he wasn't
wearing his hat.

They'd gone, left him there to die. The memories
of those few tense moments jolted Spur back to
reality. He grabbed his hat and looked around.
Vincent and Maddie had taken the money, his
revolver and the buckboard. He'd have to walk.

He didn't know how far it was. They'd probably
driven for about a half hour. Maybe a few miles.
He trudged along the trail. It was covered with so
much loose dirt that his feet sank to the ankles as
he pushed ahead. Thirsty, well aware of the dull
ache in his shoulder, Spur walked back to town.

He had to get his wound patched up. Rent a
horse. Buy a rifle. Get those damn thieves!

The sun was much lower in the horizon by the
time he straggled into Quintoch. No one noticed

him as they bustled about their business. Spur McCoy headed for the white house he'd noticed earlier. He hoped the doctor/barber was still there.

The door was open. A pudgy man dressed in striped pants and an open-collared shirt looked at him.

"Gunshot wound? Don't see many of those around here," he said cheerily.

"Just plug the leak. I got work to do." Spur slumped on the chair the doctor motioned him toward.

"Okay, okay. You should rest until at least tomorrow, but I got a feeling you won't."

The doctor removed Spur's shirt and inspected the wound. "Pretty clean," he said, leaning over him. "Went through high up. No major damage." He grabbed a small bottle.

Spur grunted as the whiskey seared his exposed flesh.

"Where'd you get this hole? How'd it happen? No shootings in town today, was there?"

He winced. "No. Just do it!"

"Okay, okay!"

The plump man wrapped a bandage around Spur's shoulder and tied the ends tightly together. "That should keep you in good shape. But don't do any wrestlin'. You hear?"

"Yeah." Spur gave the man a dollar and headed for the livery stable.

Ten minutes later he'd bought an old Navy revolver, ammo and two hanks of rope. He rode out of town, heading back for the place where Vincent had buried the money.

He felt pretty good, all things considered. The

buckboard's tracks leading east were clear but he didn't see a second set that indicated Vincent and Maddie had gone back to town. They were out there—somewhere.

He rode west on his rented horse for another ten minutes. "Whoa!"

The horse stopped and looked around, bored.

The flat impression of the buckboard's wheels headed toward him and veered off to the north.

North, Spur thought. The train?

He kicked the mare's flanks, jolting her into a gallop. The bare ground flew by as he followed the fresh ruts. They were probably going to try to stop the train somehow, he thought, and remembered the sight of the smiling young girl seconds after she'd shot him in the shoulder.

What a pair they were.

A line of trees up ahead showed the path of a small stream. He splashed across it. The horse was eager to drink but Spur couldn't take the time. "Soon, girl," he said.

The long, monotonous railroad tracks stretched out before him, fading into the distance on the flat prairie. Vincent and Maddie weren't in sight.

Cursing, he urged his horse to a fast walk. Not many features broke up the terrain. Clumps of trees and waist-high bushes grew sparsely. But he saw the remains of an abandoned house about a mile away.

It sat near the tracks—on his side. The perfect place for the two of them to wait for the train. Spur galloped up to it for a half mile and slowed his horse to a walk.

The sod house had long ago lost its roof to the

blinding sun, wind and rain, but its walls were seven feet high. He pulled out his rifle and held it ready with his right hand, keeping the reins in his left.

The horse's subtle movements made his shoulder complain but he blocked out those feelings. He had too many other things to think about.

Spur warily approached the old house.

"It'll never come."

It was Maddie's voice.

"Yes, it will. I'm pretty sure I remember what the conductor said. Should pass by here before dark."

They were on the other side of the house. He quietly rode up to it and dismounted. Spur tied the reins to a crumbled brick and checked his revolver one last time. Fully loaded.

"Land sakes, Vincent, can't you keep your hands to yourself?"

Spur padded along the far wall.

"Not with you lookin' so pretty, my dear."

"Vincent, not now!"

"Come on, you little cutie! Didn't I make you a rich woman? Look at all the money!"

He heard the sounds of boots shuffling in the dirt. Spur waited.

"Oh, all right." Maddie's voice was resigned.

"That's the spirit! Now you just let me eat this for a while."

Spur turned the corner. The side wall was shorter. He inched along it, rifle ready, slowly working his way toward them.

"Ouch! You bit me!"

"Grrrrr!"

He cleared the wall and stepped past it. Vincent Vandermeer's face was inside the girl's dress. She leaned against the sod bricks, enjoying his ministrations.

Spur fired over their heads. Vincent stumbled back, spit drooling from his lips.

"Damnit!" Maddie screamed.

Vincent grabbed the Colt stuck down his pants. Spur peeled off a shot with his Navy revolver. The slug slammed into Vandermeer's arm, ripping, tearing into his flesh. The man screamed and dropped his weapon.

"Goddamn!"

Maddie bent toward the Colt.

"Don't, girl," he spat. "Unless you wanna be next!"

The girl shook her head and straightened up. "Whatever you say."

"You shot my firing arm!" Vincent said, rubbing the bloody wound.

"Be glad I didn't kill you!"

They'd set the buckboard across the tracks, probably hoping to stop the train, give them some story and hop on. The four large money bags sat on the ground near its rear wheels.

"Planning on going somewhere?" Spur asked.

Maddie clenched her fists. "I knew this wouldn't work! I knew it the minute I—"

"Shut your mouth, girl!" Vincent yelled. He rubbed his wound, his face twisted with pain.

Spur stared at Maddie. "Got any more surprises in your dress? Where's your derringer?"

She sighed and reached into her voluminous skirt.

''Gently—gently pull it out and throw it to me. If you try anything you'll wish you hadn't.''

Maddie extracted the tiny gun and tossed it to him.

''Kick my revolver over here. Now!''

She frowned and stabbed her boot at the downed weapon. It skittered two feet on the sand.

''Farther!''

Maddie's next attempt sent it behind him. ''Good girl,'' he said sarcastically.

''Damnit! It hurts!''

''Yeah.'' Spur grabbed the Colt and stuck it into his empty holster. ''Walk to the other side of the house. Both of you!''

The despondent pair did as they were told. Spur followed them closely, switching his aim from one to the other. The horse stood patiently in the shade.

''Alright, Maddie. You should enjoy this. Tie him up!'' He threw a coil of rope at her.

''Gladly!'' She caught it and set to work. ''I never done anything like this before.''

Spur guided her. The girl worked with gusto. Her skirt flew around her as she wrapped the rope around Vincent Vandermeer's wrists.

''I told you all along!'' Maddie said to him.

He closed his eyes. The dark stain on his right arm slowly spread out. ''Hurry up, Maddie!'' he yelled. ''I'm bleeding to death!''

''Come on, Vincent, you've cut yourself worse'n that shaving in the morning!''

Finished, she stepped back, almost proud of her work. Spur examined the knots. They seemed fine.

''Now it's your turn.''

Spur bound the girl's wrists. He helped both of

them into the back seat of the buckboard. Then he hauled the money sacks into it as well, tied his rented horse to its rear and set off for Quintoch.

"I'm never going to take another train ride with you!" Maddie said.

"Shut up!"

"And you're a lousy father!"

An hour later Spur spotted Deputy Watson walking into the sheriff's office just as he was driving up to it. "Watson! Get Andrews out here! Now!"

"Okay!"

The man disappeared. Sheriff Andrews came out and stared at him. "What's this all about?"

"I got two for you," he said, pointing to the man and woman on the front seat. "They robbed the Kansas Pacific." He lowered his voice. "I have the money too. Lock 'em up!"

"Okay, okay."

Andrews and his deputy hauled the thieves into the jail. "You come by later and tell me all the details."

"Will do."

Spur drove the Quintoch County Bank. He hauled the four bags inside and watched as the president placed them in the vault. Once they were safely stashed there he dropped off the horse and the buckboard and went to the telegraph office. He wired a short message to General Halleck saying they'd been caught and the money recovered. Exhausted, he trudged over to Annabelle's house.

It was just getting dark as he knocked on the

door. He was looking forward to some home cooking.

The young woman opened the door and peered out at him. He felt better just seeing her. Annabelle was the prettiest woman for miles around.

"Sorry, drummer; I don't wanna buy anything." She started to close it.

Spur grabbed her wrist. Annabelle giggled and pulled him inside. She looked at the blood stain that plainly showed on his shirt.

"You're hurt! What have you been doing?" she asked with genuine concern.

"Business. It's fine; got it patched up. But I'd kill for supper."

Annabelle smiled. "Only if you promise you won't run out on me again."

He grinned. "I promise."

"Okay. I was just going to start cooking. Why don't I heat some water so you can take a bath?" She wrinkled up her nose. "Think you could use one."

"Okay. Won't you join me?"

Annabelle laughed. "It's too small. Besides, I have some cooking to do."

Soon Spur was luxuriating in an iron-clawed tub of sudsy water. He kept his shoulder high and dry but scrubbed the rest of his hide, freshening it for the lovely lady who hummed as she chopped, sliced and cooked in the kitchen two doors away.

Scrubbing trail dirt and sweat off his body, Spur remembered the Quintoch killings. He'd taken care of the train thieves but his job wasn't done yet.

The washroom door opened. Spur turned toward it.

"Sheriff, Sheriff Andrews!" he blurted.

CHAPTER TWELVE

Jonathan Andrews laughed as Spur sloshed around in the tub. "Relax, McCoy." He grinned.

"Well, okay." He sat upright in the sudsy water.

"I know all about you and Annabelle. Just wanted to stop by and say that the two you brought me are safe and sound. The man looks like he's ready to kill the girl and vicey-versa."

"I see." Spur relaxed. "That's good to know."

He shrugged. "What can I say about what I did to you? It was stupid. Sorry I locked you up."

"No problem." Spur stared at him. "You really don't mind my being here? Taking a bath, getting ready for your daughter?"

"Hell no!"

"You sure are one hell of a father, Sheriff Andrews."

He laughed. "And she's one hell of a girl. That's why I don't care if you fool with her. I don't want her seeing the idiots that come around here all the time." He winked. "Better be getting back to work. Old Missy Forster found her buggy missing. She swears it's been stolen, but she always forgets where she's left it. Enjoy yourself!''

Spur shook his head as the sheriff closed the door.

Soon he was digging into Annabelle's cooking. She sat watching him, amused. Spur didn't waste time talking. He just ate.

The fried chicken was scrumptious. He wolfed down four pieces, had two helpings of the peas and carrots and four cups of coffee. When she showed him the chocolate cake Spur nearly fell off his chair.

''You're a fine woman, Annabelle!'' he said, watching the thick slice fall onto his plate. Nearly an inch of fudgy frosting covered the dessert. He ate it slowly, savoring every rich morsel of her handiwork.

''You like it?'' she asked.

He tried to answer her with his mouth full. Annabelle watched him in amusement.

When he'd finished, Spur pushed back from the table and slapped his belly. ''Best meal I've had in years!'' he said. ''Now, come on over here!''

Annabelle went to him and wiped a chocolate smudge from his lower lip. ''Still have room for me?''

''You can bet on it.''

They went to her bedroom—a confection of lacy pink curtains, antique dolls and even a few books. Annabelle's bed was a huge canopied contraption.

''Looks like a man could get lost in there,'' Spur said.

''Not when I'm around.''

They undressed each other, throwing off various

pieces of clothing, eager to see each other's naked body. Stripped to the skin, Spur rubbed his bandaged shoulder and watched as Annabelle lowered her bloomers. She was as beautiful as he remembered—smooth skin, firm breasts, curved hips, a flat stomach and the erotic patch of hair between her thighs. And, for the moment, she was his.

"Jesus, you're incredible!"

"Come on, Spur!" She banged into him, sending Spur sprawling onto the mattresses. He groaned as his shoulder hit the quilts.

"Hey! Take it easy on me. I'm a wounded man. Remember?"

"Oh, I'm sorry." Annabelle kissed the bandage. "Is that better?"

"Yeah. Feels better all over." He took her hand and moved it between his legs. Spur smiled as she gripped him, wrapping her soft fingers around his awakening penis.

"That's nice," Annabelle said. She stuck her tongue in his ear.

"Oh, girl!"

Her hand moved up and down, hardening him. Spur gritted his teeth and gently pushed the woman onto her back. He fit his knees between her legs and gazed down at her.

"Annabelle, you really are—"

She touched his lips. "Don't talk, Spur. Not now. We have better things to do!"

"Right!"

McCoy nodded and bent down. She squealed at the hot contact of his tongue on her left breast. He licked around her nipple, rousing it until it stood up. Groaning, he pushed her breast into his mouth and sucked.

It was delicious, Spur thought as he feasted on the globe of soft flesh. He slipped it out and attacked the other one, chewing lightly on her nipple until Annabelle was squirming beneath him.

"Do it, Spur!" She said. "You make 'em feel so good!" Annabelle grabbed his head and moved it back and forth between her breasts, urging him to satisfy her desires.

He looked up at her. "Just tell me if you don't like it, Annabelle."

A laugh spilled out of her throat. "And you tell me if this isn't your cup of tea!"

The woman scrambled out from under him and turned around so that her head was at his crotch. Surprised, Spur looked at her lovely bush. He knew what was coming. He knew that any second she was going to—

"Ohhh. Oh! God, Annabelle!"

Her mouth was warm and fluid. She worked him over, bobbing up and down, taking him, taking all of him in her lust-crazed heat.

"Jesus!" Spur looked down to watch her happily sucking away, then moaned and burried his head between her legs. He spread her lips and tongued her delicate opening. The musky taste exploded on his tongue. Spur lapped at her clitoris, stabbing his tongue against it, banging it back and forth and enjoying her grunts. His moustache meshed with her pubic hair as he ate.

They happily licked and sucked each other, forgetting everything else, sinking into a world of sex. Annabelle used her throat incessantly, taking him to the hilt again and again. The pleasure increased within him. Soon Spur felt the tightness in his testicles, the danger signs of too much excitement too fast. He started to lose control.

She moved faster.

"Maybe you better stop that!" He gently pulled her head away.

"Okay!" She wiped her lips and gasped for breath. "Do it to me, Spur McCoy. Do it!"

He crossed his arms, grabbed her waist and flipped her around on the bed. Annabelle sighed as she sank into the quilts. She spread her legs and reached up to him.

"Gimme gimme gimme!" she said.

He got into position and thrust forward, sinking into her liquid fire. Spur grunted at the tight penetration. He pushed deeper and deeper until she'd taken every thick inch.

Annabelle flopped around on the bed as he transferred his weight to her. Their bodies were connected. Spur felt her breasts crush against his chest. Kissing her sucking lips, he withdrew and pushed.

He wanted to go slow. He wanted to stretch out their pleasure. He wanted to give her orgasm after orgasm before his last, final drives into her body. But it didn't work out that way.

Spur was too excited by the woman. He pumped between her smooth thighs. Their hip bones banged together as he pleasured Annabelle. She broke the kiss, turned her head to the side and gasped at his masculine thrusts.

"Oh hell, Spur; ram me!" Her voice was soft.

"What was that, Annabelle?" He slowed down. "What did you say?" All he could see was the fire in her eyes.

"Ram me."

"Louder!"

"Damnit, Spur; ram me!"

He pulled out to the limit and slammed into her. Annabelle groaned as their hips slapped together. She bit his neck.

He grimaced and rode higher into her, rubbing his erection against her clitoris. Annabelle shivered at the intensified sensations coursing through her body. Her hands locked around his waist. She met his thrusts, pushing her hips toward him, impaling herself on his penis.

"Oh. Oh. Oh!"

Harder. Faster.

Annabelle exploded. She shook through a tremendous release, lips wide, huffing and moaning. Her fingernails drove into his back, urging him as her world melted.

Spur stared down at the orgasming woman. The lust on her face, the intensity of her passion aroused him even further. He drove blindly into her. He was too close but he didn't care. He bucked and arched his back.

McCoy shut his eyes and roared as his seed rushed into her. His body spasmed, jerked backward with each spurting thrust. His release went on and on. Annabelle's groans mixed with his own as Spur drained himself deep inside her body.

He ejaculated one last time, grunting at the incredible feeling, then collapsed into a sweating heap on top of the woman.

His brain fried from the sex, McCoy was dimly aware of Annabelle panting beneath him. He grabbed her shoulders and pressed his lips to hers, thrusting his wet tongue into her mouth until they both had to stop for breath.

"Spur McCoy," Annabelle said dreamily between gasps. "I'll—I'll cook for you every day."

He kissed her again and drifted off into a wonderland of soft feminine skin.

A half hour later, rested, refreshed from their exertions, Spur and Annabelle slowly dressed. She looked at him as he hauled up his pants.

"Let me guess—I'm not the first woman you've ever bedded." Her eyes twinkled.

"You're right about that. But you're the best."

Annabelle smiled. "Really?"

"Really."

She looked at the rug. "Can't—can't you stay the night? We could have lots of fun together. We could do it again and again and again!"

"Sorry, Belle. I have work to do."

"Belle. No one's called me that since I was a little girl." She reached behind her and buttoned up her dress. "I like hearing it from you."

"I sure like saying it—Belle." Spur stuffed his feet into his boots and grabbed his hat. "I'll be seeing you again." He tenderly looked at the woman.

Her face was dark. "You mean before you leave?"

"Yeah."

Annabelle finished the buttons and turned fully to him, hands pressed against the smooth material that covered her stomach. "And when's that?"

Spur smiled. "Not until I find the man who's been doing all the hanging in this town."

She shivered. "I don't know if I want to wish you good luck or not."

He kissed her, a lingering, tongue-lashing kiss. With difficulty, Spur pulled his head from hers. "I know. Thanks for dinner—and everything."

Annabelle nodded as he walked to the bedroom door.

Don't turn around, Spur told himself as he went through the big house toward the entrance. He heard her feet pattering along the floorboards.

"Spur!" Annabelle called, her voice breathy.

"Yes?"

She hesitated, so he looked at her.

The woman's lower lip trembled. "Hell." She forced a smile. "Good luck."

"Thanks."

It was dark outside. Light showed through thousands of panes of glass. Figures moved inside the buildings that lined Oak Street. So many people. And he wasn't any closer to finding his man.

Spur shook off the lethargy that had invaded him ever since he'd finished with the young woman. He looked down the long avenue that led to Main Street. Where was that murdering bastard?

There was one place to start looking again. The Prairie King Saloon. Maybe he'd talk to the remnants of the 14th Regiment.

The crisp night air awakened him as he strolled along the dust. Spur stretched his arms, lifting them high above his head and locked his hands around his wrists.

He entered Main Street and turned toward the saloon, passing drunken cowboys, rich ranchers, a few fancy ladies scurrying to work, women with screaming babies, and fresh-faced young couples enjoying the evening together.

Spur surveyed every face, looking for the visage of a killer as he made his way through all the humanity. He didn't know how he'd recognize it or even if he could. But he'd try.

Something hard and cold pressed against his back.

"Don't think about going nowhere!" a low voice said.

CHAPTER THIRTEEN

Spur froze. The revolver's muzzle dug into his lower back. Alcoholic breath blasted around his head.

"I thought things like this didn't happen in Quintoch," he said wryly.

"Shut up! How much money you got?" his attacker said. The voice was grave.

"Why? You interested in a loan?"

"Don't mess around!" The barrel nudged against him. "I gotta get another drink and I'm flat broke. How much you got on you?"

"Check for yourself. My moneyfold's in my front pocket. The right pocket."

"No. You pull it out and hand it over!"

Spur was silent.

"Damn you! Do it!"

"You want it so much—you go for it." Spur was playing with him. This wasn't an experienced, cool thief. And he wasn't about to get his money.

"Well, well...." The man thought about it. "Awright."

The pressure eased on his spine. Spur elbowed his unseen attacker's ribs and wrestled the revolver from his right hand. He spun and smashed his boot into the man's groin. The chunky man howled and doubled over in pain.

"Thanks for the weapon." Spur pushed it into his pants.

"Damnit!" The would-be thief lifted his head. "Damn you!"

McCoy plowed his fist into the man's jaw, sending him reeling back.

"Come on; you've got an appointment."

Spur grabbed the man's belt and hauled him a half block down to the sheriff's office. Jonathan Andrews nearly spit up his coffee as he looked at him.

"Thought you were with my daughter!" he said.

"Was. This joker tried to rob me." Spur pushed the groaning man to the ground. He landed on his butt and shook his head.

"Sam? Sam Feingold?"

"Take care of him, would you? I've got something that needs my fullest attention."

"Sure, sure McCoy." The sheriff stared down at Feingold, shaking his head. "Mighty big crime wave we're having."

"Right."

"Well, come on, Sam. Sleep it off."

Spur grunted and walked outside. Just what he needed—more distractions. But nothing could distract him from his mission.

He got a whiskey in the Prairie King Saloon and glanced at the back tables. Just two men sat there. He recognized one of them—Mike Hughes, the one

who'd been talking about being scared the night of
Lester Field's murder. The one who'd knocked on
the sheriff's door that night. The one with the
nervous tic below his bushy eyebrows.

McCoy frowned. Could be. It just could be.
Maybe the man couldn't stop himself. Maybe he
had to kill to root out some old, ugly problem that
had been brewing in his gut since the war.

He walked over to the table.

"Damnit, where's Feingold?" Hughes said. He
flipped off his hat and mopped his sweating
forehead.

"Easy, Hughes. You know sometimes he's late
getting away from his wife."

Hughes fidgeted with his bottle. "Never been
this late before."

"You lookin' for Sam Feingold?" Spur said.

Hughes turned to him. "Who wants to know?"

McCoy smiled. "He's at Sheriff Andrews' little
hotel. Your friend got drunk and tried to take my
money."

Hughes rose to unsteady feet. "You accusin' my
friend—"

"Calm down, Hughes!" the other man said.

"Don't worry," Spur said. "No one got hurt.
He's sleeping it off, nice and safe in the jail."

Mike Hughes slumped into the chair.
"Well—well" he stammered.

"So he's okay. Nothing's happened to him."

"Obliged for that. I'm 'Ketch' Ketcham," the
smaller man said. "Ol' Hughes here's been pissin'
in his pants."

"I just don't wanna bury Feingold too!"

"Heard there's been some trouble in this town."

Spur slid easily into a chair at the table with the men. "Hangings, wasn't it?"

Hughes sucked down a swallow. "Yeah." He wiped his chin. "Four of 'em. All my friends. All dead. There's only three of us left."

Spur turned to Ketch as if he needed an explanation. "We wuz all together during the War."

"I see. You think someone's still fighting that war against you boys?"

"Hell, I don't know." Ketch drummed his fingers on the table.

"Ketcham here thinks it's co—co-" He scratched his head. "What'd you say?"

Ketch weakly smiled. "Coincidence."

"Right. But it ain't. They're all our friends. Andrews ain't done a damn thing about it!"

Spur could see the anger and fear inside the man. He was convinced that neither Hughes nor Ketcham had anything to do with the hangings. It was truly and outside party. "Guess there's not much to go on. A town this size—"

"Blast this town!" Hughes downed the last of his whiskey and hurled the bottle onto the floor. He didn't wince as it smashed into a fine layer of sparkling crystals. "I'm gonna leave. Just pick up and go somewhere else."

"Might be a good idea," Spur said.

Ketcham frowned. "He's been saying that for a week now. I'm starting to believe him. But that won't do nothing, Hughes! If someone is after us—all of us—he'll track us down. No matter where we go."

Hughes put his head on the table and banged the boards with both fists. "I know! I know!"

"Nice talking with you," Spur said as the man went into near-hysterics. He tipped his hat and took his drink to the bar for a refill.

"Hey, got something to tell you!"

It was Gussie Granger, wearing an even tighter, smaller lime green dress that covered less of her than ever.

"Yeah? What is it?"

She shook her head. "Not here! Come on!"

He was surprised when the whore dragged him outside onto the front porch. At least she didn't expect him to screw her, Spur thought.

"Okay." He leaned against the pillar five feet from the front door.

"How much'll you pay?" she eagerly asked, her face glowing in the diffused light seeping from the saloon.

"What's this all about, Gussie?"

"Sheriff Andrews tole me all about what you're really doing here. You're not looking to start a saloon!"

He sighed. "I see. So you know something about the hangings?"

She nodded, then shook her head. "Hell, I don't know. It could be." Gussie lifted her eyebrows.

It was worth a gamble. "Five dollars."

"Jack Hastings. Know him?"

Spur shook his head.

"He works at the hardware store. A young 'un. He's the one who came to see me the other day and didn't do nothing to me. Remember I tole you about him?"

Spur nodded.

"Well, he saw me today—middle of the

afternoon! Woke me up and everything. Said he
was supposed to be eating lunch." Gussie fanned
her ample bosom. "That boy's weird, I tell you! He
made me do all kinds of things—but not like you
might think." She paused for effect.

"Go on," Spur said.

"Made me pretend I was his mother, living on
the plantation. Made me rattle on about the
magnolias, pecan pies and the squirrels." Gussie
shook her head. "He never tole me what it was all
about, but I got a sneaking suspicion it's something
about his mother. I think she's dead."

Spur frowned. He vaguely recalled the man in
the hardware store. "How old would you say he
was?"

Gussie shrugged. "I don't know. Twenty. Twenty-
one. A babe in arms, 'cept that's the last place I had
him. It's something to do with the War. He must've
been a little tyke back then."

His mind churned, digesting the bits of
information. Jack Hastings. He's from the South.
"Did he say where you were supposed to be during
all this?"

She rolled her eyes. "Georgia. Somewhere near
Atlanta."

He gave her a five dollar bill. "Thanks, Gussie.
You've made me a happy man."

"I have?"

"You have. Now get on back in there and earn
some more money so you can go on home!"

"Yes sir!"

He slapped her behind as she scooted inside.

Jack Hastings sat alone in his house. Though the

place was small it was crammed with silver candlesticks, broken furniture, charred paintings and every other piece of his home he'd been able to recover after the Northerners had ransacked it.

When the bluebellies had left, Jack had wandered around the burned mansion for two days. No one came near; no one came to help. He slept in trees and ate whatever food he could find in the cookhouse. Once in a while he forgot and ended up near the porch. The boy had tried to avoid seeing his dead parents but he couldn't push them out of his mind. He couldn't pretend nothing had happened.

Everything had happened. All at once the life he'd known had been shattered. His father and mother lay cooking in the sunlight. Even his pet pony, the one his father had sent all the way to England for, had disappeared. He waited and cried and waited.

Finally an aunt of his from Augusta rattled up in a rickety wagon. Four other men were with her, distant cousins of his, Jack remembered. She'd heard about what had happened and had come to see what was left—if anything. She was surprised to see that Jack was alive and well.

"God was good to you," Aunt Esther had told him. "Now it's time you were good to God."

She'd packed every salvageable item onto the wagon and took the boy to her home—an austere, lonely horror. For six years, until he turned 18, his aunt forced him to be her servant. He washed, painted, scrubbed, waited on her hand and foot. The old biddy had hated her sister, Jack's mother, and she took it all out on him.

One thought kept Jack going during his youth—he would avenge his parents' death. He'd kill the murdering bastards who'd destroyed his whole life.

When he was 17, his aunt suddenly died. Jack had loaded up the memories of his youth into the same old wagon and rode it across the country until he landed in Kansas. He moved from small town to small town, looking for men who fit in with his childhood nightmares.

Hastings finally settled in Quintoch and planned his revenge. He knew about the group of seven ex-14th Regiment soldiers. And a few weeks ago he'd finally started exorcising the pain.

Jack sighed and looked at the cast-iron kettle that his mother used to use for soap-making. He remembered her outside in the back, throwing fat and lye into the monster. He recalled the nose-numbing smell and the harsh results that she used to scrub the rich Georgia soil from his little body.

A knot formed in the back of his head. He squeezed his eyes shut. No, he shouldn't have. He shouldn't have thought about old times. He shouldn't have thought about his mother.

Now it was too late. There were still three more men to go, three men between the pain and the pleasure of revenge.

His head aching, Hastings checked the carton near the door. Out of rope again? Jack sighed. He'd have to get some from the store.

Spur found the gray, blank-windowed store huddled next to the Quintoch County Bank. He didn't figure Jack Hastings would be there at that time of night—it must be around nine—but he might as well check it out.

The street was relatively quiet. This was wild frontier town, most of the locals seemed to take to their beds early. So Spur was surprised when a figure approached the store with a determined gait.

The man walked directly to the door.

"Excuse me. You Jack Hastings?" Spur yelled.

He turned around and regarded McCoy. "Ah—ah yeah, that's me."

"You're not opening the store, are you? I sure could use some ammunition. Someone told me you were the man to see."

"Ah—sure. Just a minute." He pushed his hands into his pockets. "Dang! Hell, I gave the keys back to the owner. Guess not."

Spur shrugged. "Okay, I'll come by in the morning. When you open?"

"Eight."

"Thanks."

Spur turned and moved down the boardwalk. He settled back on a hitching post and casually looked down the street. Jack Hastings walked into the darkness, slamming his fists against his thighs.

He disappeared.

CHAPTER FOURTEEN

Spur hurried down the darkened street after Jack Hastings. He found him again, wandering past a brick house. Hastings was taking his time getting home, McCoy thought, as he faded from shadow to shadow.

Soon the big, opulent houses were in the distance. Hastings kept on walking, rubbing the back of his head. Spur heard the man groaning softly into the night air.

He finally turned a corner and moved down a half-block past small, single-story dwellings. Jack Hastings walked to a squat house and went inside.

Seconds later the glow of kerosene light yellowed the solitary expanse of curtains.

He must be home, Spur thought. He found a comfortable tree to lean against a half-block from Hastings' place and pressed his back against the thick trunk. Might as well watch him for a while.

Jack Hastings seemed harmless enough, not exactly the shooting, killing kind. But then again, the killer had hung the four men.

Rope. Working in a hardware store Hastings certainly had access to plenty of rope. So did most of the other citizens of Quintoch, for that matter. But Gussie's vivid account of Jack Hastings' peculiarities made him wonder. The Civil War. Georgia. A plantation. A possibly dead mother. And the murders of the Kansas 14th Regiment, all of whom had helped bring down the South. Did they all fit together?

Possibly.

Spur yawned and hunched over. The tree was dark; anyone glancing outside wouldn't see him. He settled in for a long night, peering at the small house in the distance. The house that may hold a killer.

Three hours later the light went out. Jack Hastings must have gone to sleep. His knees and back were cramped from the awkward position, so Spur stood and rubbed his eyes.

Hastings might have been planning something that night when he'd met him at the hardware store. Maybe he'd scared the man off.

Spur watched for another hour until well after midnight. Still nothing. No sign of movement, no lamps being lit. Hastings was apparently fast asleep.

You should be too, Spur told himself. Nothing's going to happen here tonight. He just had that feeling. Spur shook his head and walked toward Jack's home, moving slowly. McCoy peered at the tiny structure. It looked grey in the thin moonlight. Weeds had grown up around it save for a patch that led straight from the street to the covered porch. Nothing seemed unusual.

Sighing, Spur walked back to his hotel room. He had a bad feeling about Jack Hastings.

Spur opened his eyes with the dawn. He heard horses and buggies moving in the street below his window. The sounds of Quintoch coming to life roused him. McCoy went to the pitcher and basin and splashed his face. The water stung him with its coolness, washing away the last traces of sleep. Alert and ready for anything, Spur strapped on his holster, put on his boots and hat. He'd just wear his fine shirt, vest and pants. No coat today, he'd decided—too hot for that.

McCoy opened his hotel door and was greeted by Kay Fordham—pointing a rifle at him.

"Kay!" he said. "Watch what you do with that thing!" Spur eased the barrel to the side.

She laughed. "I'm sorry, Spur. I was just gonna knock."

"Uh-huh." He eyed her curiously. "What brings you to my room—with that?"

If she'd been any other woman she would have blushed. As it was, Spur saw a faint tinge of color on her cheeks. "I wanted you to show me—"

"How to use it?" Spur said, blocking the entrance to his room. "You own a rifle and don't know how to shoot?"

"No, no, no. I shot lots of rabbits and things when I was a little girl. My father always wanted a boy. But I don't know how to clean a rifle."

Spur nodded. "Fair enough. But why come to me? You must know lots of other men in town."

Kay bit her lip. "Most of 'em won't talk to me. They won't come near me—afraid I'll turn their wives against them." Kay delicately pushed her left hand against Spur's chest. "Hey, can I come in?"

"Okay." He made room for her.

"Thanks." She barrelled in like she owned the place. "I do want you to tell me what to do with the rifle, but I was also hoping you'd clean me out." Kay Fordham said the words without the slightest hint of coquettry.

"Sorry, woman. I gotta eat some breakfast and go to work. Unless you'd like to cook for me."

She smiled. "Sorry, Spur. I—uh—wouldn't want to hurt my chances later on. My cookery's that bad." She handed him the rifle. "So what do I do?"

He carefully explained the simple procedure to her, telling her how to break it down, what to oil, how to wipe it off and reassemble the rifle. Kay eagerly absorbed every word, nodding every once in a while.

"Got it. Thanks. You're a real pal!"

Spur flinched. "You look like one, but you sure don't talk like a woman."

"I know. There's only one time I act like one." Kay touched his thigh. "You sure?"

"I'm sure." He gave her back her rifle. "I've got to be going. Nice seeing you again, Kay."

"You too."

He walked her down the stairs. Two men hooted as they entered the lobby.

"Lookit that!" a grizzled man said, slapping his knee. "Old Kate-the-freight-train done nagged herself a live one!"

"Hell, Marcus, he won't be breathing long after a

few hours with her." His friend was an earlier version—same beady eyes, same double chin, same jug-handled ears.

Spur looked at Kate.

She straightened her back. "That's just Jim Fletcher and his son. I'm used to it—from them."

"Whoo-whee!" the codger exploded into laughter.

McCoy walked up to the father and son, who sat on a couch near the front desk. "You got a problem, mister?"

Fletcher controlled himself. "Hell no. Looks like you do, though." He poked his son in the ribs.

"That's no way to talk about a la—" Spur bit off the word, sending the two men bouncing up and down on the leather couch with guffaws.

"Spur, it's okay!"

"Now look, Fletcher," McCoy said. "I want you to apologize to Miss Fordham."

"Heh heh. Whew! Apologize to her? I'd as soon kiss Sheriff Andrews!"

"Yeah, or his daughter!" Marcus Fletcher threw in.

Kay Fordham stomped up to them, shaking the rifle in her hand.

"Don't!" Spur said.

She transferred the weapon to her left hand, made a tiny fist and blasted it into Jim Fletcher's jaw. The connection was surprisingly solid. "Shut up!" she screamed.

The man's head jerked back from the blow. He stopped laughing and rubbed his chin.

Kay glared at him, face flushed, panting.

"This means we're married?" he joked as his jaw slowly turned bright red.

"You want more?" She shook her fist at him.

"Alright, alright! Jeez, Kay!" Fletcher said. "Just kidding around! Nothing serious like!"

"Come on, Spur; let's get out of here."

She grabbed his arm and led him out of the hotel. Spur went with her, admiring the woman's spunk. Not many females would have done what she'd just done.

"You probably think I'm some kind of monster," Kay said as they stood on the front porch. She leaned her rifle against her right shoulder.

"No, Kay. I think it's admirable that you showed that man the, ah, error of his ways."

"It was so womanish of me!" Kay shook her head.

"Womanish? You—I—I can't think of many women who would have hit that man. Even if he was saying things like that!"

"Not what I mean," she said. "I lost control. I let myself go like a foolish girl." She moved the rifle to her right hand. "I hope I didn't embarrass you, Spur."

He laughed. "No, not at all, Kay."

"Good." She pecked his cheek. "Guess I'll go home and try to figure out this rifle. Nice seeing you again, Spur."

"Likewise, Miss Fordham." He nodded and turned toward Sheriff Andrews' office.

The suffragette was some kind of woman, though Spur didn't know what kind. If there were just a few more like her they'd carve the west into hospitable land that much faster. But how could the men handle them?

Spur sighed and went into the jail. The sheriff was busy wolfing down a plateful of scrambled eggs, bacon and biscuits. He waved as McCoy sat in the chair opposite his desk.

"Your daughter's cooking?" McCoy asked.

Andrews nodded, chewing. He grabbed a tin cup of coffee and splashed some into his mouth.

"She sure knows her way around a stove." The smells rising from the steaming food made his stomach grumble. He realized he hadn't stopped for breakfast in his hotel's dining room. A whirlwind in feminine form had distracted him.

"What's on your mind, McCoy? Any more train thieves?"

He glanced back at the door to the jail proper. "Nope. You know a Jack Hastings?"

"Hastings. Hastings." Andrews scratched his scalp and chewed half a biscuit. Melted butter dripped down his chin. "I've heard of him," he said, his mouth full.

"Know anything about him?"

Andrews shook his head. "Can't say I do. Never been in any trouble far as I can remember. Why?"

Spur reached toward the plate. "Do you mind?"

The sheriff smiled and wiped his lips.

"Thanks." The bacon was still warm, and Spur enjoyed its crisp saltiness. "I have a feeling he's up to something. One of the girls at the Prairie King told me a little story about this Jack Hastings. I'll check up on it."

"And you let me know." Another forkful of eggs slid into the sheriff's mouth.

"I will."

Spur went to the hardware store. It wasn't open yet, so he grabbed breakfast at the communal dining table in his hotel. He was alone save for a gun-packing youth who almost looked old enough to shave.

He barely noticed the brown-haired kid as he devoured the food.

"You ever shoot anybody?" the boy asked him.

Startled, Spur looked at him. "Why?"

The boy shrugged. "Just wondering." He fingered the thin hair on his upper lip. "But did you?"

McCoy shrugged. "Yeah. And it isn't fun."

"My daddy's dead. He got hung. Last week." The youth's face was expressionless.

"Sorry to hear that, boy. What's your name?"

"Clemons MacArthur, sir."

"Well, Clemons, I'm gonna find the man who hung your daddy. Don't you worry about that!"

The boy looked down at his plate. "I hope so. Momma took sick and I have to look after the place, coming in here to eat."

Spur finished his meal and glanced at the grandfather clock in the corner. Seven o'clock. An hour to go before the hardware store opened.

The ache in his knees matched that in his head, but Jack Hastings continued kneeling on the floorboards, praying his heart out.

"Yes, mother, I'm doing your will. I've done it to four of them so far."

His face squeezed up. "But mother! I couldn't do it last night! I didn't have any rope! And that man scared me. I coulda been caught. Might've been taken prisoner by the bluebellies or killed."

Jack lifted his head. "What's that? What're you saying, mother?" He sighed. "Well, it's too soon. I can't do it yet!"

He listened to the shrill voice in his head, accusing him, berating him for his lack of faith.

Hastings looked into space, his eyes glazed. "Alright, mother. Tonight. I'll hang another one tonight." He banged his hands against his skull. "Can't you make this headache go away?"

Spur watched the hardware store all morning long. He even went in to buy some ammunition he didn't need, just to see Jack Hastings in the light. The man seemed pleasant enough. Spur confirmed he didn't have a trace of a Southern accent, but a man could do that if he tried hard enough. Lots of former Georgians and Alabamans had lost their former accents since the end of the War.

He checked the stolen money he'd recovered. It was still safe and sound in the Quintoch County Bank. Then he took up his post again, waiting for night, waiting for Jack Hastings to make his move—if any.

It was just getting dark when Spur heard feet shuffling up behind him.

"Mister?"

It was Clemons MacArthur, the youngster he'd eaten breakfast with.

"Yeah?"

The boy looked at his feet, then at Spur's holster.

"My momma says I'm the man of the family now. I have to protect her. So I was wondering if you could teach me how to shoot."

Spur smiled down at him. "Maybe you should learn how."

"I know guns ain't toys and all that," Clemons said. "And I'm a fast learner. My father taught me how to do practically everything. else. Now he'll never teach me."

The poor kid, McCoy thought. "I'm real busy right now," he said.

Clemons turned down his mouth. "Okay. I figgered you'd say that."

"But try Sheriff Andrews. He might help you out. In fact, I'll ask him to. How's that?"

"Sure. Thanks, mister!" His eyes shined up at him.

Spur started to feel like a hero. "I'll talk to him today. See you, kid."

"Great!" Clemons ran off.

Two hours later, Jack Hastings walked out of the store and locked it. He had two coils of rope in his right hand. Nothing suspicious about that, McCoy thought, but he followed the man as he walked down the street.

Hastings kept clutching the back of his head, rubbing it. The rope swung back and forth in his arm as he moved. To Spur's surprise Hastings didn't head for home, but turned down a side street. He walked up to the front door of a large house and knocked.

Spur shrank back in the darkened street and watched.

A woman answered it and, reluctantly, it seemed, invited Hastings in. McCoy was too far away to be able to hear what they were saying. The front door closed.

He darted across the street and walked up to the window. Mike Hughes came into view.

"Who the hell's that, Angela?" Hughes asked, arms crossed on his chest. "You invitin' your boyfriends over to the house now? You gonna take him into the bedroom?"

Angela Hughes was calm. "Now, dear, don't get all riled up. This poor man needs help with something or t'other."

Hughes scratched his chin. "Go find someone else!" He turned and walked out of the room.

Mrs. Hughes smiled at Hastings. "I'll try to talk some sense into him."

"Would you let me?" Jack smiled at her and went in through the doorway.

Spur watched the woman circle around on the floor. A dull thud issued from inside the house.

"Mike?" Mrs. Hughes asked. "Are you all right?"

Jack Hastings lunged for her, hammer in hand, the rope coiled around his neck. "He's just fine, Angela."

"What'd you do to him?" She backed away from the man. "What have you done with my husband?"

"Nothing."

"You stay away from me!" she shrieked. Mrs. Hughes grabbed a cobalt blue vase from the mantel. "I'm warning you!"

"Now, now. None of that!" He advanced on her. "That isn't ladylike behavior!"

Angela hurled the vase. It sailed three feet and smashed onto the floor. "Don't hurt me! Please, don't hurt me!" She stared at the hammer.

"Maybe I won't if you keep your mouth shut!" Jack walked up to the terrified woman.

She nodded, eyes wide.

Hastings tied her hands behind her back. He worked quickly, methodically knotting the rope. Jack pushed her into a chair and secured her ankles to the thick oak legs. "You just sit there and have a good rest, hear me?"

"Don't do this!" Angela Hughes said. She broke into sobs. "Leave us alone!"

"I don't wanna do nothing to you. It's your husband, Angela. Your murdering, bastard husband! He's the one I'm gonna kill!"

"No!"

He grabbed a lace doily off the table and stuffed it in her mouth. Hastings pushed it so deep that the woman couldn't spit it out.

"If you scream again I'll kill you too! Maybe if you were from the South I might forgive you. But you're just a goddamn Yankee. So shut up!"

Spur watched the scene with growing unease. He fought off the impulse to rush in and free the woman. He had to catch the man in the act of hanging. That was the only way to connect him with the earlier killings.

"I'll be right back," Jack Hastings said. "And when you see me your husband'll be dead."

Angela struggled against her bonds as Hastings walked into the other room.

Spur moved to the next window. Mike Hughes lay unconscious on the kitchen floor. Hastings whistled as he tied the noose. He hurried through it but soon got a serviceable knot.

''Who said the War was over?'' He slipped it over Hughes' head and pulled it tight.

CHAPTER FIFTEEN

His head ached.

Nearly blinded with pain, Jack Hastings opened the door and started hauling the unconscious man out to the woodshed. He'd checked out the small building a few days ago and it seemed perfect. It had an open beam just the right height for his purposes. Sure, it wouldn't be a fast death, but soon Mike Hughes would be dead just the same. Then only two of his parents' murderers would still be alive.

Blood pounded in his brain. He gasped at the intensity of the internal torture and halted. "Soon, mother," he whispered. "Soon you can rest in peace."

He got the man fully out of the kitchen.

Crouched outside the window, Spur watched Jack Hastings prepare for his latest hanging. There was no immediate danger. He'd have to move the still unconscious man.

Sure enough, Hastings dragged Mike Hughes to

the kitchen door and opened it. Spur slid up beside it and waited. Hastings backed out, dragging the man.

He'd seen enough. Spur stepped from the shadows. "Going somewhere, Hastings?"

Jack stumbled and dropped the man's torso. "Who—what're you—"

Mike Hughes groaned. His right arm moved aimlessly in the dirt.

"The War's over, Hastings. It's been over for a long time. Stop fighting it!"

Hastings held his hands toward Spur in earnest. "No! He—he murdered my mother and father! He torched my home! He killed my whole life!"

"Him? This man?" Spur shook his head. "No. You can't be sure of that."

"He did! I'm just finishin' up the job!" He grabbed his head. "Damn, it hurts!"

"Come on, Hastings." Spur gripped him and pushed the man into the house. Once in the parlor he patted the man down. He wasn't armed, just crazy. "Untie the woman!" he said, shoving him toward her.

Angela Hughes, still bound to the chair, looked up at the two men in fear.

"It's okay, Mrs. Hughes," Spur said. "I'm not with him. I'm on your side."

She struggled against her bonds, shaking her head, trying to spit out the doily that gagged her. Spur pulled it out and stroked her hair. "Okay now?"

The redhead gazed at him, then nodded.

"Good. Get to work, Hastings!"

"Damn! Oh, sorry about that, ma'am." He

moved around her and loosened the knots, his face expressionless, distant.

For safety's sake, Spur drew his Colt .45. He glanced toward the kitchen. Just outside Mike Hughes stirred, sat on the bare earth and rubbed his scalp. He looked into the house and saw Spur.

"What—what happened?" he asked.

"What's that around your neck?" Spur asked.

His hands went to it and felt the rope. "God-damn!" Hughes grabbed at it, struggling, finally loosening the knot. Then he threw the noose behind him. "You mean it was Jack Hastings? From the hardware store? He's the killer?" Hughes pushed himself to his feet and stormed into the house.

"Take it easy." Spur turned back to watch the woman's untying.

"Like hell!" Hughes thundered. "That asshole just tried to kill me!"

"You're still alive."

He pushed past McCoy, looked at the man who was busy untying his wife, cursed and ran into the bedroom.

"You about finished?" Spur asked.

"Yes, sir." Hastings pulled the end free. The last knot dissolved and the rope slapped onto the floor.

Angela Hughes stood and moved to the wall, staring in fear at the young man. Her face was pale and tight, her throat bobbed up and down as she nervously swallowed.

"Hughes, get in here!" Spur shouted.

The man appeared, holding his old Army rifle. "It's time you got a taste of your own medicine, Hastings!"

"Michael!" Angela shouted.

"I'm gonna plug that bastard," Hughes said, gripping the weapon with both hands. "If you try'n stop me, mister, I'll shoot your head off, too!"

"Kill him!" Angela viciously shouted. "Kill the son of a bitch!"

"Calm down! Both of you! I'm a federal law enforcement officer," Spur said. "I'm taking this man into custody. If you stop me I'll have you arrested for—"

"Piss on you!" Hughes swung up the rifle and blasted a hole through the wall, ten feet from Hastings.

Angela covered her ears as the explosion reverberated in the parlor. "Kill him!" she screamed.

"That's enough!" Spur tackled Mike Hughes. The two men banged onto the couch, knocked it over and spilled onto the floor. The rifle skittered away from them as Spur grabbed the man's hands.

"Grab the rifle, honey!" Mike yelled.

"Too late for that!" she said. "He's getting away!"

Spur tried to break free but Hughes clutched him with his left hand and vainly tried to punch with his right. Spur rolled on top of him and smashed his fist into Mike's face. He broke from the groaning man and sprang to his feet.

"He's gone and it's all your fault!" Angela screamed. She attacked him, slapping at his face and shoulders.

Spur ignored her, grabbed the rifle and started for the door. The ex-soldier crashed into him.

"I warned you, didn't I?" Hughes said.

McCoy swung around and planted his fist on the

man's chin. The woman screamed as her husband reeled back, lost consciousness and flopped onto the couch.

"You killed him!" she said, rushing to him.

Spur snatched the rifle from his hands. "He'll wake up. Keep him here!"

"I—I—"

He was out the door.

"Mister! That man grabbed the horse out back and rode off that way!"

Spur squinted. The young boy he'd spoken with during breakfast stood beside his own mount.

Clemons patted the horse's rump. "You can borrow her if you want!"

"Thanks, MacArthur. I owe you one!" The kid must have been watching him. Smart boy.

Spur slid onto the saddle and kicked the horse into a gallop. It easily responded and soon he was racing toward the south into the night.

Jack Hastings couldn't have gotten far.

The horse was lazy, he thought. "Come on, girl, faster!" Hastings' stomach was queasy from the pain. His brain felt like someone had driven a hair pin clear through his skull. It pounded in rhythm with the unwilling horse's hooves.

Fast. Faster. Come on!

He didn't know what went wrong. Nothing should have gone wrong! He had him. He'd almost done it when that man showed up. The same one who was there when he tried to get the rope from the store last night. The same one who bought a box of ammo from him that morning. Damn him! He'd been watching him.

Hastings enjoyed the cool air blasting against his face. It seemed to make the pain in his head subside somewhat. It didn't matter anymore. It didn't matter what happened to him. He'd done most of what he'd set out to do.

He looked around him. The moonlight showed a stark, barren landscape. Not much place to hide anyway. He might as well stop and wait for the man who was surely following him.

The image of his dead parents flooded through him. The anguish surged anew through his veins. The years of toil at his aunt's feet sprang into life.

No. Damnit, no!

He jabbed his heels into the horse's flanks. "Move!" he yelled.

Hastings sighed as the horse reluctantly obeyed his command. He never had had much call for the beasts, but this one sure was coming in handy.

He'd get away, somehow. He'd get away and hang the three murdering bluebellies. Then, and only then, would he be free. Even if they killed him for doing his duty he wouldn't mind. He'd die in peace and happily join his mother and father in heaven.

"Faster, girl!" he screamed, fearing he'd hear the sound of a rider behind him.

Spur slowed his horse. No sense in racing in the wrong direction. He couldn't tell if the man had continued on in a straight line, and the night was so dim he couldn't see any details on the earth below him.

He reined in the boy's mount, jumped to the ground and lit a lucifer match. The tracks were there, plain and crisp on the dew-covered earth. Hastings was still heading south. But to where?

Spur continued on, occasionally glimpsing a freshly trampled plant that showed the man's trail.

Jack Hastings was a strange character. Why would he set out to kill another man without bringing along a weapon? Some sort of protection? It didn't make sense, unless it was part of some elaborate revenge plan.

Or unless he was out of his head.

McCoy continued following the invisible trail, stopping at frequent intervals to check the tracks with a match or a torch twisted from dried prairie grass.

On the sixth such stop Spur cursed. The ground was hard-packed, as if it had been flooded recently and dried to an impenetrable crust. There were no hoof prints in sight.

He walked in circles around his horse, fanning out farther and farther away. He came across nothing but an owl resting on a scrubby bush.

Jack Hastings had vanished.

He sighed. He had two choices. Keep on going and trust his instincts, or wait until sunrise to start tracking the man again. Spur walked back to his horse, who stood shifting its weight as if eager to be on. The mount whinnied at the flame before he crushed it out with his heel.

He'd lost time trying to pinpoint Hastings' tracks. The man could be miles ahead by now. Or he could have stopped and was now snoring away on the ground. Somewhere out there.

He slid back into the saddle. No time like the present, he thought, and kept going in the same direction.

The moon began to set in the west. The enlarged orb off his right shoulder seemed to temporarily give off more light. Soon Spur saw a dark track stretching into the distance.

A trail.

Hastings must have been heading for it. He was a local man and knew the surrounding area. Though Spur didn't have any idea where it led, he urged the horse along the well-worn track for five minutes, lit a match and searched the dirt.

Fresh horse prints. Hastings must have come this way.

He rode south until dark blue light tinted the eastern horizon. It was dawn.

Tired from the saddle, weary from lack of sleep, Spur surveyed the territory as the day began. It was flat, featureless prairie land. A few ranches— big, fenced-in spreads—broke up the monotony. But the clean tracks led straight down the trail. Hastings—if it was indeed his horse—hadn't stopped.

A half hour after the sun broke over the horizon, Spur reined in his horse. The hoof prints veered to the right, down a lane between white picket fences.

He followed them, peering at the golden-tinted ranchhouse in the distance. Maybe Hastings had spent the night there.

The ranchers seemed to be asleep. Spur halted his horse at a hitching post outside the farmhouse and was pleased to see an ungroomed mount standing there. He tied up his mare, watching a plump woman in a bonnet and a calico dress heading toward the henhouse with a basket.

"Ma'am?"

She kept padding by.

Spur ran up to her. "Excuse me, ma'am," Spur said.

The ranchwife turned to him and pleasantly smiled. A pair of spectacles was perched on her nose. "What can I do for you, stranger?"

"Did a man ride up here last night? Someone you don't know? Maybe he asked for food and lodging?"

She smiled. "Yes. Came in—land sakes, it was late. James put him up in the spare bedroom."

"Can I see him?"

"You a friend of his?"

"Sort of."

"Of course. Go in through the front door, down the hall and up the stairs. It's the first room on the right. Now I have to be getting those eggs. Good morning!" She trotted off toward the coop.

Spur sprinted to the two-story house, quietly opened the door and went in. He walked over the rag rugs that covered the wooden floors and eased up the wide stairs. There was the door. McCoy turned the knob and pushed it open.

It was a plain room, with a huge oak bed covered with smooth quilts. It hadn't been slept in. Nearby was a small stand with the indispensible ewer and basin. But Jack Hastings wasn't in sight.

Spur's guard went up. He drew his Colt and stepped into the room.

"Don't!"

Jack Hastings sat in the corner, knees folded, an antique flintlock rifle in his hands. He stared at McCoy's weapon.

"I'll shoot you!"

"I thought you only hung men, Hastings."

"I shoot 'em, too. Did lots of shooting in the War fighting against the North!"

Spur shook his head. "You weren't in the War, Hastings. Remember? You were too young."

"Yes I was!" Hastings said. He stood, supporting his back with the wall. "I killed lots of them Yankees. Shot and hung 'em!" Sweat squeezed from his forehead; dark half-circles showed below his eyes.

"And you're still hanging men. Aren't you? You hung Lester Fields."

Hastings shook his head and showed his teeth in anguish. "Never heard the name."

"You know him. And you tried to kill Mike Hughes last night. I stopped you."

He choked out a laugh. "I see. You're trying to fool me." Hastings' eyes grew dark. "Hell, you're one of them Yankees too!" He pushed off from the wall.

"Put that rifle down," Spur said. "You're gonna hurt yourself."

"No I won't! But I'll hurt you. I'll shoot you! It's loaded and everything!" Hastings smiled. "I don't have a rope but this'll have to do! Just hold still and let me kill you." He pointed the rifle in Spur's direction, but his aim wavered back and forth.

"Give it to me." McCoy tentatively took a step forward. "You can't win."

"No, Yankee!" Hastings fired the primitive

weapon. The lead ball slammed into the wall. Blue smoke filled the air, mixing with the explosion. The recoil sent him stumbling backwards.

"What in hell's going on here?" an old man in a nightshirt yelled as he appeared at the door.

"Nothing I can't handle," Spur said. "We'll be out of your hair soon."

"You can't go and shoot up my house!" the farmer said. "Hey, that's my rifle!"

"I'd take cover if I were you, sir!"

"Okay, okay, sonny." The man mumbled and ducked out of sight.

Still dazed by the explosion and lack of sleep, Hastings pulled the trigger again. Nothing.

"A flintlock only fires one round. It's over, Jack. Come on."

"No!" He rushed for the door.

Spur smashed the butt of his Colt into Jack Hastings' neck and banged the top of his head. The muscular youth screamed and dropped to his knees. He moved his face between his legs and started crying.

McCoy shook his head and retrieved the rifle. He laid it on the bed, helped Jack to rise and escorted him down the stairs.

"My rifle alright?" the rancher asked.

"Yeah!"

It was over.

CHAPTER SIXTEEN

Hastings was silent during the long trip back to Quintoch. Spur looked at him occasionally, taking in the man's sad eyes and slumped shoulders. He moved gently up and down on the saddle, his hands bound before him, emotionless.

"You know it wasn't right, don't you, Hastings?"

No answer.

"Even if you did lose your parents and the plantation during the War, that doesn't give you the right to kill innocent men! How can you be so sure they were the ones who did it?"

No response.

"I figured as much." The man was out of his head. It was that simple. Spur sighed and hurried toward town.

Almost two hours later they trotted past the houses on the outskirts of Quintoch. Jack Hastings looked up at the Hughes house and shook his head.

"No more," he said, his voice soft and raspy. "I won't get any more of 'em."

"Haven't you done enough?"

"There's still three more!"

"Look, Hastings, terrible things happen during wars. The Civil War wasn't any different. I'm sure you suffered as much as anyone. But you didn't have to hang those men."

"No more." Hastings raised his face to the sky.

They moved out to busy Main Street.

Not far to the sheriff's office, maybe a half mile.

"That him?" a man shouted.

"Yeah! It's Hastings! The one who tried to hang me last night!"

Spur recognized Mike Hughes' voice behind him.

"We don't want any trouble," McCoy yelled.

"We do!"

A bullet whizzed past Spur. He turned around. Three men stood with their weapons drawn, staring at Jack Hastings. Women and children scattered.

"Put your guns away, boys. I'm taking this man to jail. He'll get a fair trial."

"No way!" Hughes bounded up to him and grabbed his horse's reins. "I've got some unfinished business with that man!" He hefted a huge coil of rope.

"Lynching's murder. You wanna get what's coming to Hastings?"

Hughes laughed. "No judge'd blame me! Now ride outa here, McCoy! I could shoot him but I wanna do it up right! Just like he did to my friends!"

"Yeah! Let's take him to the walnut tree!"

Three other men joined the group of ex-soldiers. Spur sighed. At six-to-one he didn't like the odds.

He wrested the reins from Hughes' hands and

pulled Hastings' mount beside his. "You're talking crazy, Mike!"

"Enough! Let's get him!"

The six men rushed Hastings' horse, screaming, hands outstretched. The mare bolted at the surge of humanity, whinnying and rearing up on her front legs. Jack Hastings fell off the saddle and rolled on his shoulder, his hands still tied.

Spur fired over their heads but the men didn't flinch. They grabbed Hastings' arms and legs and started hauling away the dazed man.

Cursing, McCoy dismounted and attacked the mob. He grasped Hughes' waist and hurled him away, then punched a few chins and took a fist to his left shoulder.

The old wound surged back into memory, the bullet hole magnifying the pain. He winced and drove into them again, succeeding in knocking two of them on their butts. Hastings broke free from the men and aimlessly ran right into Sheriff Andrews' arms.

"Now you boys stop it!" Andrews said, holding Jack. "This man's in my custody now."

"Like hell!"

The bloodthirsty mob surrounded him.

"We ain't gonna stop until we've finished what we came here to do!"

"Hastings hung four men! He's gonna kick from a rope before the day's done!"

"Stand back, Andrews, unless you want it too!" Hughes threatened him.

The sheriff sighed, released Hastings and walked toward Spur. "They're not too friendly this morning," he observed, folding his arms on his chest.

"That's one way to put it."

"He's the one that hung all those men?"

Spur nodded.

"Well, at least that's over."

"Not yet," McCoy said, watching the fracas. "We should try to stop them."

Andrews chuckled. "Don't see how we can. Don't think anything would. They're out for blood." The sheriff drew his revolver and fired into the ground a yard from Mike Hughes' feet. The man didn't even notice. "See what I mean?"

"Yeah."

A group of citizens flooded into the street, watching the fight.

"Hey, this is better'n Dr. Marvel's Traveling Patent Remedy Show!" one young man yelled.

Annabelle appeared among them, saw Spur and ran over to him. "Are you still in one piece?" she asked, looking at him with concern.

"Oh, Annabelle, he's all right," her father said.

She looked at him. "I just wanted to—"

The violence intensified. The men kicked and punched Hastings, screaming their lungs out.

"What?"

"I'm just glad that you're—"

"How's that?" Spur shook his head.

"Glad you're not hurt!"

He smiled. "Me, too."

Annabelle turned to the sheriff. "Father, aren't you going to stop them?"

"We already discussed that, me and your beau."

"I see."

They all turned to watch. "You won't charge

them with anything, will you, Andrews?'' Spur said, taking the hand that Annabelle thrust into his.

"Don't rightly know. I completely understand why they're doing it, though I don't approve." He paused. "Maybe there won't be any witnesses willing to testify against Hughes and the rest of them."

Spur frowned. "That's not exactly by the book."

"True. But in this case . . . ."

Clemons MacArthur waved to McCoy from the crowd.

"Andrews, see that boy over there?"

"Yep. That's Clem's son."

"He helped me out. Loaned me his horse. Think you could give him a few shooting lessons? Teach him how to safely handle a revolver?"

The sheriff laughed. "Of course! Hell, you saved my butt from these folks. That could be me out there."

"Thanks. I'll be right back." Spur retrieved the boy's horse, who'd wandered over to the nearest trough, and took her to him. "Thanks for the loan, kid." He handed him the reins.

"Sure. Anytime! I'm glad you caught the man who murdered my father." The boy's face shined with admiration.

"With your help. The sheriff said he'd be glad to show you how to shoot. Oh, and one other thing." Spur dug into his pocket and took out two silver dollars. "For the use of your horse, son." He flipped them to him.

Clemons MacArthur watched the shimmering metal discs arc up and then hurl downward. He caught the coins and squeezed his fingers around them. "Thanks, mister."

Spur tousled his hair.

Sheriff Andrews grabbed the rope from Hughes' hand. "Ain't no more hanging gonna go on in this town!" he said.

Mike Hughes started to argue, then nodded. He wiped a trail of blood from his lower lip. "Whatever you say, sheriff!" He took a breath and rejoined the others who were still whacking away at Hastings.

"What d'ya say we go over there in the shade? It's powerfully hot this morning," Sheriff Andrews said to McCoy.

They walked under the porch of Millison's Grain and Feed, purposely avoiding watching the altercation in the street.

"Thanks, McCoy. I couldn't have done it without you."

"That's my job, Andrews. That's my job."

Annabelle laid her head against his good shoulder and sighed. "How about some of my cooking?" she asked.

Spur's eyes lit up. "Annabelle, I'd love it!"

CHAPTER SEVENTEEN

"You've done what you came here to do. Now git on home before I lock you all up!" Sheriff Andrews shouted.

The exhausted, bloody men walked off without comment, revealing a battered Jack Hastings lying in the middle of the street.

Annabelle gasped and turned her head.

"Is he still alive?" Spur asked.

The sheriff felt his neck. "Barely. Come on, McCoy. Let's get this man to Doc Lemmon."

"I'll wait for you at home," Annabelle said. She kissed Spur's neck and hurried off.

The two men carried the bleeding killer to the doctor's office.

Stu Lemmon was grim. "I was expecting you," he said. "Lay him down there."

"Not a pretty sight, eh?" Andrews asked.

Hastings gasped on the table. His breath was hollow, tortured. He lay motionless, his eyes closed, life oozing out of the dozens of wounds that fists and boots had made all over his body.

The doctor opened his shirt and lowered his pants, examining him.

"What do you think?" Spur asked him.

"It's bad." Lemmon wiped his forehead. "He won't last much longer. In fact, I'm surprised he's still with us."

Hastings gurgled sickeningly. A long, drawn-out hiss of air escaped between his lips. He was dead.

"That's it." Doc Lemmon said. "Nothing I could do. Sorry, Jonathan."

Andrews shook his head and looked at Spur. "We should have stopped them."

"No, sheriff."

"Why in hell not?"

"They would have killed us. You saw them! They were blinded with hatred. And if we did manage to stop them they would have stormed the jail. Mowed you down to get at Hastings." Spur shook his head. "It was a no-win situation. Two men alone can't stand against a dozen with murder on their minds."

"I guess you're right. At least there won't be any more hangings in my town."

"Yeah." He glanced at the lifeless body. "Your daughter's waiting for me."

"Yeah." Sheriff Andrews touched Spur's arm. "Make her forget what she saw this morning. Okay?"

"Sure."

"I'm pretty tired, Annabelle," Spur said as he sat down at the dining table in her house. "Didn't get any sleep last night. Too busy watching Jack Hastings."

"You poor man!" she clucked. "Bet you're hungry, too. Right?" She held a platter full of steaks under his nose.

Spur smiled. "That's a fact."

"Then I guess you'll just have to eat these." Annabelle set the plate down in front of him.

"You're a good woman."

He dug into his food. The meat was hot, liberally seasoned with pepper and salt. He ate without talking, thinking about the morning's events.

When he'd arrived, Annabelle was depressed, anxious and upset. After she saw him, the young woman came back to life. Soon she had acted as if nothing had happened that morning. Spur made certain he didn't bring it up.

Spur shook off the memories so he could fully enjoy the meal she'd prepared for him. Annabelle ran from the kitchen to the dining room, bringing coffee, hot buttermilk biscuits, corn on the cob and other delights.

She finally sat down beside him and ate.

"Thanks for cooking me this fine dinner so early in the morning," Spur said before sinking his teeth into the buttery corn.

"I was hungry, too. Besides, I never heard of a law that says you have to eat bacon and eggs for breakfast." She delicately wiped her chin. "Spur, you aren't too tired to—well, you know. Are you?"

He laughed and swallowed. "No, Annabelle. I'm not."

"Good!"

They eagerly finished their meal. As the young woman took the dishes to the kitchen, Spur went to her bedroom. Might as well have a surprise for her, he thought, and kicked off his boots.

Annabelle walked in a minute later and gasped. "Why're you all naked like that?" she asked in mock indignation. Her green eyes locked onto the thick organ hanging between his legs. "And in my bedroom! I'll call my daddy, the sheriff. He's gonna throw you in jail!"

"Take off your dress, Belle." Spur stood before her and smiled.

She threw up her hands. "Well, alright. I never could say no to a man. Especially a naked man."

Annabelle laughed. Staring at his aroused organ, she sat on the bed and unbuttoned her tiny black boots. Then she rose and opened the front of her dress, unfastening the mother-of-pearl buttons that ran down to her groin.

Spur enjoyed the spectacle of the girl denuding herself. Annabelle threw off the dress, dropped her petticoats, yanked the bodice from her torso and slid down the snowy bloomers.

"I hope you're happy!"

"I am, Belle. I am. Come on over here."

She walked to him, completely comfortable in her nudity, and pressed full-length against him.

Her skin was soft and warm. Spur groaned as his erection smashed between their bodies. He passionately kissed her, their lips searing, his tongue darting into her mouth, pushing toward the back of Annabelle's throat.

She grabbed his shoulders and writhed as their tongues fought. Spur felt her breasts pushing against his chest. He reached down and cupped her round hips, pulling her closer to him, increasing the pressure of his trapped penis.

Annabelle threw back her head. McCoy kissed her ear and trailed his mouth down her neck, across her shoulder and to her left breast.

"Oh, stranger, I don't know who you are but you sure know how to make a woman happy."

She wanted to play games? Okay, he'd play a game with her. He bit the nipple, hardening it, teasing it with his teeth. Annabelle sighed and grabbed his head, forcing her whole breast into his mouth.

They both groaned. Spur sucked it, pushing it deeper into him, savoring its womanly flavor. Sweat sprang out of his body as he worked her over.

He pulled back and gasped. "You sure have some fine ones, Belle!"

"Don't stop!" She directed his head to her left breast and sighed at his mouth-work.

Sexual heat flooded through him but he controlled himself, nipping her tenderly, taking care not to hurt her as he feasted on the delicious mound.

He finally stepped back. Annabelle looked down at his firm organ and sank to her knees.

"You—ah—you don't have to do that!"

"I know." She moaned and took him.

"Oh. Oh Annabelle, darling!"

The woman filled her throat with him.

Spur gasped and ran his fingers through her blonde curls. The woman was incredible, he thought, as she pulled up and stuffed it into herself again.

The feeling was unique and incredibly erotic. Spur felt his knees start to buckle as she grabbed his buttocks and pulled him full-length into her. She didn't choke or gag as every inch of his penis disappeared down her throat.

Spur couldn't take much of that. He grabbed her head. Annabelle willingly rose, a devilish look in her eyes, and allowed him to lay her on the bed.

"Come on, Spur!" she said.

He raised his left eyebrow. "What happened to the 'stranger'?"

"You're no stranger to me."

Spur moved on top of her. Annabelle squealed as his fingers ran between her legs, probing, parting her lips. Her opening was soft, wet and ready.

He removed his hand and rubbed the head of his penis back and forth. "Do you want it, Annabelle?"

"Yes."

"Really?"

"Yes, Spur!"

He pushed into her. She arched her back and sighed as their bodies joined. Spur jabbed and thrusted, sinking into Annabelle, staring down at her lovely face as he penetrated.

"Oh!"

"Yeah, Belle!"

He went slowly, taking his time, trying to cool the fires that burned inside him. Spur finally drove his erection into her length.

She came alive. Her eyes widened; her hands slapped onto his back. "Yes! God, it's so—so—"

"So big?" he guessed, withdrawing and plunging back into her.

"Yes! You know it is!"

In. Out. In and out. Spur held her shoulders and

pumped between her legs, moving as slowly as possible to maximize their pleasure. He kissed her again, his tongue mimicking the movement, opening her up at both ends.

Sex musk rose up and filled the air as they made love. Annabelle's canopy bed squeaked in rhythm with his thrusts. He pushed faster into her and bit her ear.

Annabelle's nails raked his back. "Ram that thing into me! Come on, Spur!"

He lifted himself onto his hands and grinned down at her. The new angle of his thrusts drove Annabelle crazy.

"Harder. Harder, Spur! Please!" Her face glowed with sexual heat.

"Anything you say!"

Their bodies slammed together. Nothing like making love to a woman, Spur thought as he moved faster inside her. Nothing at all.

Soon he was beyond all thought. His hips pumped with supernatural speed. Annabelle's groans rose to breathy cries as he drove into her again and again.

"Yes. Yes. Yes!" she chanted. Her body undulated below him; her head hit the bed frame.

Spur moved her down, slowed his penetrations, giving them both time to rest. He pulled out to the head and held it there, poised.

"Take it!" he yelled, and rammed full-length into Annabelle.

"Oh!"

He was relentless, out of control. "Jesus, Annabelle!" he yelled.

A low moan issued from her throat. "Oh no. Oh

God! Here it comes. Here it comes, Spur!''

He sped up his pumps, deliberately pushing her over the edge. The naked woman rattled and shook beneath him. She tore at her hair and clamped her thighs around his legs, squeezing his erection with her genitals.

Annabelle cried the timeless roar of a climaxing woman. Her breasts bounced crazily and flushed a bright red as she shuddered through the intense experience.

''Yeah, Belle!'' Spur shouted above her.

The sight of her pleasure, the contractions around his thrusting penis and her open lust intoxicated him.

''Join me, Spur!'' she gasped.

He pushed into her like a wild animal, holding back his orgasm, forcing her body to its peak again and again until she was panting from the effects of his work.

Her screams rose higher. ''Goddamn it, Spur! Come! Join me, you son of a bitch!''

His scrotum tightened as it slapped against her body. Spur gasped and pounded into her, oblivious of everything but her warm opening and the shining eyes below him. He yelled and slammed into her, driving deeper than he'd ever been. His crotch exploded, his nerves shattered in a warm breeze. Every muscle in his body tightened and relaxed as he drained himself deep inside the sheriff's daughter.

''Oh Belle! Oh God!''

''Shoot it!'' she said, and sunk her teeth into his sweaty neck.

It went on and on. Spur's mind dissolved. The

woman clutched him. The spurts grew shorter until he'd coated her vagina with his warm seed.

Spur slumped onto her, spent, useless. His breath blasted against her shoulder. Annabelle sighed and moaned. She ran her fingers through his wet hair.

He knew he should say something to her, about how wonderful it had been, but the words were still locked in his lust-fogged brain.

"You know something?" Annabelle muttered, her voice breathy.

"Hmmm?"

"I'll miss you."

"Mmmm."

"I guess you'll be leaving Quintoch soon, now that you've done your job."

"Uh-huh."

She grabbed his ears and lifted his head. "I don't want you to leave, Mr. McCoy!"

What could he say, Spur wondered.

Annabelle released him. He settled down on her breasts. "I'll never see you again."

"No."

"Damnit! It's not fair! I finally find the perfect man for me and he's slipping away from me!"

"I'm sorry, Belle. There's nothing either of us can do about that."

"At least I'll have my memories. They can't leave me." She stirred beneath him.

He looked at her. "I'll always remember you, Annabelle. I'll always remember the sheriff's daughter in that little town in Quintoch."

"Really?" Tears brimmed in her eyes.

"Really."

She sighed. "Well, I guess that's all I can ask for. Isn't it?"

"Yep."

They held each other until they'd cooled off in the light breezes.

The next morning, Spur boarded the Kansas Pacific train just as it left Quintoch. Riding in a specially equipped security car, he'd brought along a special cargo—four sacks of freshly printed money.

Yesterday, he'd wired General Halleck in Washington, telling him of the death of the mad hangman. Six hours later he received a reply.

His superior's response was short and terse. Spur had a new assignment, beginning immediately. He was to escort the currency shipment, stopping to deliver the money to various banks scattered throughout the mid-west. He'd be riding shotgun on the currency until he'd dispersed the last dollar bill, protecting it from any further misadventures.

The job would take two weeks, and General Halleck told him he'd already lined up another job for him when he was finished with that.

He glanced out the window as the train pulled away from the station. He saw the blonde-haired girl waving goodbye, a brave smile on her face. Sunlight glinted in her hair; the steam from the train ruffled her pink dress.

Spur lifted his hand and returned her farewell. The train picked up speed as it drove westward. He bent nearer the tiny window and strained his eyes, watching as the woman on the platform gradually diminished in size and dissolved into the moving landscape.

Don't think about her, he told himself. That's dangerous territory. Think about your new assignment, about Washington, about anything else. Don't let that pretty little woman get to you!

McCoy shook his head. It had been just another job. He'd been given an assignment and he carried it out like any Secret Service agent would do.

He should be satisfied with himself. He'd corraled two train thieves. He'd found a man who'd been terrorizing the whole town.

But he'd left something undone, Spur told himself. A job that he should have assigned himself.

A green-eyed creature named Annabelle.

Spur looked at the canvas money sacks and sighed. Some day he'd have to go back to Quintoch, Kansas.

Some day.